TAKEN
BY THE
TWINS

INTERNATIONAL BESTSELLING AUTHOR

SARAH SPADE

FOREWORD

Thank you for checking out *Taken by the Twins*!

This is the seventh book in the **Sombra Demons** series and, like the others, can be read as a standalone though it does finish an arc that began with *Claimed by the Creature* and continued on in *Grabbed by the Guard*. It's also a holiday-themed novella—beginning on New Year's Eve—and is a short, spicy MFM romance with a sprinkling of plot to lead readers toward the final book in the series.

In the books released directly before this one, readers are told that Sierra and Billie were once in a girl group in their teens with Tandy Lewis. Each grew up and moved on. Sierra — known as Whiskey Rose — is the most famous pop star in this universe. Billie, her longtime best friend, is her manager. And Tandy... well, she's Tandy.

She's also meant to be the mate to the only set of twins in Sombra: Lucian and Damien, the doppelseers who make an appearance in Billie and Glaine's book, *Grabbed by the Guard*. Powerful visionaries and seers, these twins share everything: including their essence —and their one true mate... as long as Tandy agrees.

(And she will, of course. In fact, this book—that is definitely for 18+—is full of instalove with a heroine who is flattered and delighted to be a fated mate— though she might need a minute before she's ready for *two* of them... so, like, five days? It also has the most spice of the series, including a DVP bonding scene at the end, and a heroine who is unapologetic about the fact that she'll happily bang her demon mates.)

I hope you enjoy spending the new year with Lucian and Damien—Tandy certainly will!

xoxo,
Sarah

CHAPTER 1
RED

LUCIAN

I see *red*.

In our future. In our past. Whenever the visions come, featuring my twin and me instead of any other Sombra demon in our realm, everything I see is tinged with red... and after nearly three millennia as a seer, I still don't know what that means.

And that is frustrating because, between Damien and myself, we know *everything*.

We are the doppelseers. Two male demons born of the same essence, we were blessed by the gods with the gift of sight. What I see, Damien knows. What Damien senses, I understand.

Except for *red*.

It wasn't always red. For so long, the future was shadowed. We see all, except for that which concerns my twin and me in particular, until the day it changed —and now it's all the same fiery shade hiding what I desperately want to see.

Red has meaning to my brother and me. After all, it *is* the color of Sombra. With its two moons—one gold and one dark—and the reflection of fire burning endlessly in the ash fields, ours is a shadowy world that is as red as the cast that covers my visions now whenever I focus on the single prophecy that I've waited nearly thirty centuries to see come to pass.

Damien and I together, a faceless female between us as she takes our cocks, takes our essence, takes our power... and, finally, as part of a trio, we are whole.

But while I've existed all this time by remembering the fleeting sensation of pleasure, of how it'll feel when I finally work my length inside of my one true mate's cunt instead of stroking it quickly with my hand just to find some relief, I don't see *her*. I don't know who she is. And Damien... he needs the relief even more than I do. Bottled up tightly, always on the verge of losing the last vestiges of the purple in his gaze, when my twin is sensing the twisted future for our fellow Sombrans or doing favors for the duke himself, Damien lives and breathes *red...*

Red like fire.

Red like love.

Red like *need*...

We need our mate. All Sombra males do, but as the doppelseers... we've existed longer than any other demon in our realm because our life will only truly begin when she accepts us as hers.

It's been nearly thirty centuries since our wait began. Three millennia spent expectantly—and, at long last, it's almost over.

Though a slightly different shade, red is also the color of our demon skin, when we turn solid and step out of our individual shadows. But though the female I dream of and Damien longs for is shielded from her males, one thing has always been clear to us both: our one true mate is no demon. She is a mythical human female from the legendary world of the mortals, and the reason our wait is as long as it is is because she didn't exist until a few *decades* ago.

Damien saw her in his visions first. When she was born, he knew, though we had to then accept we'd have to wait until she was mature enough to receive us, and for the matefinder spell to connect us. Even so, Damien sensed her essence before I first saw the shadows shift to red in my own visions.

In his unique way of sharing what he sees, Damien spoke of a dying ember, a spark that would ignite us both, then snuff out quickly like the fires in the fields that end up suffocated by the mounds and mounds of ash on the edge of the shadows—unless she chose to bond herself to us both.

My twin has a tendency to speak in riddles. It is a consequence of our birth. He is closer to the realm of gods than any other demon in Sombra, and he *sees* much farther than the respected seers that serve their clans.

The doppelseers serve Sombra, though our loyalty is first to Duke Haures, the ruler of our world. We are the ones who pushed him to oust King Yelios after we sensed that our mate would be a mortal—and that Haures would be the first to claim one of the human females as his own.

That happened three decades ago; both Haures's claiming of his duchess, and the certainty that mine and Damien's female finally existed. After an eternity, the bound *Grimoire du Sombra* with the matefinder spell inside its pages did what I knew it would: it gave Haures's mate the ability to call the duke to the human world, setting into motion the prophecy we made so many centuries before.

Susanna found him. She summoned him, and she mated him. Once our female has the grimoire in her possession, she will do the same for us.

Gods willing, that is. Damien and I saw the dark-haired female as she welcomed Haures into her body and her heart. When it comes to our own mortal, there is no certainty that she will.

But she *must*. If not for my sanity, then for my brother's...

Every demon exists with one purpose in mind: to choose a mate, love them, claim them, and share their essence with them. Our essence is designed to be given away, but only once; unless, of course, you are a rare demon twin like Damien and me. It is our most fervent wish to find our one true mate, though some demons settle for any female that will have them.

Damien and I have always known that we must wait for *her*. For the one soul who would eventually welcome two males in her heart *and* her body. No one else would accept the doppelseers as her future, and if she doesn't... we might not have one.

Because if she doesn't accept the both of us? Damien will perish, and without my twin, so will I.

We are the doppelseers. Our powers are both vast and unique, but they are not limitless. Damien saw that Haures would find his mate in a dark-haired human female who would rule by his side in Mavro while hiding behind the shadows that Haures sacrificed in her name long before she ever existed in her mortal world.

Haures is a bondmaster. Only by combining his rare gift to sense and manipulate bonds with our ability to see what is to come were the three of us able to create the matefinder spell all those centuries ago. But while he sacrificed his shadows to have enough magic to create the *verus amor* to open a portal into a magicless world, he used his inherent strength to rule Sombra while enforcing his first law.

The human world has always been off-limits. Since Damien saw that an alliance between our realm and theirs would lead to the ruination of Sombra, Haures was careful to keep the rift between worlds closed— until the future duchess, Susanna, called him to her, setting into motion the events that would lead to our mate calling us to her side.

She would be the seventh. A powerful number in the realm of magicks, the seventh female would be *ours*... and apart from the color red, that was all I could see about our one true mate.

Of the two of us, I see the clearest. I always have, but never when it involves Damien and me. Then, my visions are as confusing and hazy as my twin's, and I'm left with a vague impression of my human, the sense that time is slipping right through my claws, and the color red.

It is the gods' way of ensuring that the doppelseers are not forewarned, though after nearly three millennia, I have learned ways around it.

That is why, for the last ten gold moons or so, we have taken every chance we can to visit the small town of Nuit, on the farthest edges of Sombra's shadows. In this quaint village, there are two human females who live with their demon mates: one who is with spawn, and the other who has recently chosen to stay in Sombra with her mate, Glaine of Duke Haures's guard.

The female who is with spawn is not the one spoken of in the prophecy. Only the first mortal female who bears a child which will be part-human, part-demon is mentioned, and that pale-haired female is currently with the Nuit healer, Azazel.

We have perhaps one gold moon until her child is here, or even two if the gods favor us with extra time to greet our mate. After all these centuries of waiting, we're on the cusp of seeing long-awaited prophecies unfold: both the one that worries Duke Haures, and the one that means everything to me. Our visions always allowed that the female fated to belong to my twin and I would be the seventh mortal to use her human magic to cast the *verus amor* spell and visit Sombra.

But if the spawn is born first and there is no more Sombra...

No. I will find her. I will claim her.

And I will do so for Damien—and for my people.

This eve, we have requested to meet with two of Haures's guards: Dagon, who no longer serves Haures as he's moved to the human world to be with his mate; and Glaine, head of Haures's guard who resumed his position after being left in chains and put into the duke's infamous dungeons in Mavro. Knowing that they would only bring their mates if they were also invited into the doppelseers' cabin, we are all crowded around a fifth demon as he bows his head over a large scrap of parchment that Haures gave us for such the occasion.

The fifth demon is Malphas, a golden-eyed artist who once called Nuit his home. Like Dagon, he lives in the human realm with his mate, the pale-haired human, Shannon, who is fated to be the first mortal to birth a demon spawn in Sombra.

Malphas doesn't often come to Sombra. Only when his human mate needs to visit with the healer. The visits are more frequent now that she is at the end stages of carrying her mate's spawn, preparing to welcome the child into both worlds, but since she is not yet laboring, we sent out the invitation for Malphas to visit us as well.

Two cycles ago, I waited until Damien rested, then marched out into the shadows myself. I don't carry a weapon, not like Glaine and his shadowkiller blade, gifted to him by Haures himself. I have no need to since my white eye allows me passage among the darkest shadows for a small amount of time.

Besides, over the millennia, I have had need to risk facing the creatures who lurk in the depths. Without the ashbalm flower to keep the bond open between my twin and me, he'd be fully demonic in no time. And while I can only imagine how much clearer my visions would be if I had two purple eyes, the mark of a mage, I don't regret anything I've done to protect my twin.

I stewed him the leaves of the ashbalm, adding the flower itself to my concoction, then watched him drink. It's no demon wine. Damien won't admit how foul it tastes, but if the result is that I keep him with me, I will brew the drink for him every time.

The benefit to giving Damien the ashbalm flower? It extends his powers, and with the bond strengthened between us, I see better.

The last time we tendered an invitation to the two human females—who act like they are kin, though there is no shared blood between them—I saw something peeking through the red. A hint of green, a color so unusual to Sombra that I had to search for the word to explain to Damien what I envisioned, plus white skin, a shade we know all too well, having been in a centuries-long agreement with Duke Haures.

After discussing it with Damien, we came to the conclusion that, at long last, our female's essence was reaching through realms to find us. With the *Grimoire du Sombra* still in the human world, it was our hope that the magic in the book would lead it to land in our future mate's grasp.

That is all we can do. Before, whenever Damien and I could see the future and know who the next human mate would be, Haures had played his part in making sure the book fell into their hands. He had a human male on earth that he used, a male he met through the duchess, and the servant placed the book specifically in the reach of the female who needed it next.

From the mortal Shannon all the way to Glaine's mate Billie, the matefinder spell has been used to fulfill the main prophecy that has shadowed Duke Haures's millennia on the throne.

But we don't know who our female is. We couldn't arrange for her to receive the grimoire—until the red faded, and we realized it only did when Glaine and Dagon's mates, Billie and Sierra, were near enough for Damien and me to read their essence.

Before the guard bonded to his human, we tendered them an invitation to our lair. As unique as our powers, bespelled by the doppelseers before our mage powers faded until all that was left was our sight, the cabin made of ashwood travels all of Sombra. We are never still. Never in one place. But because of the prophecy, we knew that Glaine's female was important.

What we didn't know? Was that, when we met her, she would be *red*.

Not on the outside, of course. It was her essence that caught my attention, but all it told me was that— at some point—she knew our mate.

Then Sierra visited, and the sensation grew.

Damien could feel it, too. And though he's been quiet lately, lost in his own head, he offered to open himself up to the clan artist to illustrate what the both of us see. I agreed. We'd have to do it together, after all, letting Malphas inside our twin bond so that he can draw the flash of *her* face we glimpse whenever the other two human females are near.

If they know her, if they recognize her, we will be one step closer to claiming her.

A name. It starts with a name…

Billie and Sierra are human, not demon. Their essence belongs to their mates. Since they are not of Sombra, our ability to share the twin bond with them won't work, so we had no choice but to involve the artist.

Luckily, he was more than willing to help us while the healer tended to his mate.

Damien senses the whisper of our mate's essence more easily than I do. The logical twin, I need to *see*. Much more in tune with his demonic nature, he *feels*— and however he does it, it works. Using the four colors of *giz* we gathered for Malphas—red, green, white, and black—he draws on the parchment until a stunning rendering of a red-haired female with red lips, green eyes, and colorless white skin is pouting back at us.

"There," Malphas murmurs, setting down the chalk. "This is the female that the doppelseers have put in my head."

"Red," whispers Damien, his white eye glowing much brighter than usual.

"Fucking hell," explodes the female with the braid. Dagon's mate, Sierra. "That's *Tandy*."

Tandy.

"Tan-dee." I taste the name between my fangs as I murmur it softly. I like it. "You know this female?"

"Know her?" She waves her wee hands at herself, then Glaine's female, Billie, she of the big gold hair, a similar color to Malphas's craftsman-colored eyes. "We used to be in a band with her!"

Glaine's female leans around Malphas's shadows. "Holy crap. That's the spitting image of her."

I frown. "The drawing is of a smiling female. She is not expectorating."

They share a look that makes it clear that there was some sort of miscommunication between their Sombran and my native grasp of my tongue.

Dagon's mate shakes her head. "I don't know about all that, but that drawing... it's Tandy. I'd recognize her anywhere."

"She is your friend?" I ask.

"Yeah... I wouldn't say *that*."

Damien's white eye is still glowing brightly. Before the other males in the room can notice, I feed a little of my essence down our shared bond to bring Damien back around while closing it off from Malphas.

Damien's purple eye flashes, and my twin snarls around his fangs as his magic overwhelms him once my essence settles in his veins. "A creature with no legs, who crawls on its belly in the dirt and takes that which doesn't belong to it... that is who you think she is."

Dagon's mate wrinkles her strangely smooth brow. Without the ridges I expect from a fellow demon or demoness, it's unprotected and more colorless than a Sombran's solid shape or shadows. "What was that?"

It wasn't a prophecy. Courtesy of the doppelseers' twin bond, if Damien was using our innate gift to take his visions of the future and share them in the only way my twin can, I'd be aware of it even if I didn't understand what he sees. But while my main power is seeing things before they happen and putting them plainly if I can, Damien can simply understand things about those he reads.

And what he read from Dagon's mate is enough to have his white eye flaring again.

"A *snake*, Sierra," offers Glaine's mate, emphasizing the human word. "He's telling you that he's picking up on you calling Tandy a *snake* in your head."

Snake. I do not know this word. It must be a human translation, but based on what Damien said to her, I imagine one of the groundcrawling *jamda* creatures that slither on their bellies as they nip at a demon's heels while he's in his solid form. Solid black except for the glowing white eyes that all shadow creatures have, the *jamda* is a nuisance.

And this human says the same of my female?

"Are you an empath?" I ask her. "Can you read others?"

"Who, me? Nah." Glaine's mate shakes her head, all that human hair bouncing wildly as she does. "I'm just an old pro at reading my way around a contract. It took me a while to figure it out, but Damien's riddles are like the Sombra demon version of legalese. A lot of words to say a little, and once I figured that out, deciphering what he says sometimes became a lot easier."

Glaine beams. "That's my Billie. Such a clever mate."

She is. At least, for a human, she is, but I already knew that. At Duke Haures's request, when Billie and Glaine were traveling on the edge of the shadows, working their way toward Nuit, we kept an eye on their journey.

And then I saw red, and Damien sensed that the sixth mortal to bond with one of our kind would lead us to the seventh, and we moved our home out of the shadows before inviting the human and her guard to stay with us so that we could get a better read on her essence.

She is clever... and for the first time in centuries, I feel hope.

Hope that the time to take our mate is here at last.

Hope that, with Damien's hold on our shared essence growing more tenuous by the cycle, she can save him.

Hope that she can love us both, and possibly even save *me*.

And then, only when the doppelseers are whole at last, can we hope to save Sombra from the fate we foretold millennia ago—and that, with the upcoming birth of the first human-demon spawn growing closer and closer, we might not be able to avoid.

TANDY

Whenever Jared Turner starts texting me out of nowhere, I immediately have this need to check and see what my old friend Sierra's up to.

It's been like that ever since the two of us—Jared and me—fucked-up our lives so badly, we both lost something super important to us. For me, it was my spot as a member of the all-girl singing group Thr33-peat. And, of course, Jared's relationship with Sierra was over the second he convinced me that she'd grown too successful for his level of fame as a boybander, and that he chose me over her.

It's been twelve years since I stupidly, *stupidly* believed him. Twelve years since I fell into bed with one of my best friend's boyfriends, and twelve years since my life imploded for the first time, but definitely not the last.

I loved him. Stupid to admit it after how everything went down, but I did once. With Sierra working toward becoming Whiskey Rose, I knew our days as 'One', 'Two', and 'Three' were numbered. She was going to break out and go solo, and already believing I was being left behind, I turned to Jared. He turned to me. We 'fell in love', though I eventually had to admit that I'm the only one who really did.

I was twenty then. My rep as the sultry redhead with the soprano voice only got worse when news broke that I slept with Sierra's long-term boyfriend behind her back.

I was the slut. The homewrecker. The replacement.

Sierra's career took off almost right away. She wrote a song after she dumped Jared, and once 'Heart Barely Used' went, like, triple platinum, everyone in the fucking world knew who Whiskey Rose was.

She's the most famous pop star of our generation. And Tandy Lewis? I'm the most infamous tramp in our circle.

I'm thirty-two now. Once Sierra became Whiskey and Jared regretted getting some side action, he's spent the last twelve years chasing her. He wants her back desperately, though he'll never admit he will, and whenever he starts chasing *me* again, the reason why inevitably leads back to her.

I don't have time for this BS. I have a party to get ready to go to, and it's the first thing I've had to look forward to in ages.

Christmas when you're on tour—no friends, no family, and decade-old gossip still following you wherever you go—really sucks. My hotel has a Christmas tree in the lobby and old-fashioned carols piped in through the halls, but that was the extent of my celebration. I got drinks with a couple of girls in the show on Christmas Eve, but when Moira—a one-hit wonder who peaked five years ago—asked me if I've ever had a threesome with Jared Turner and Whiskey Rose, I paid my part of the tab and went back to an empty room.

That wasn't the plan. Though I've never been able to outrun that rep, it makes finding a bedmate for the night pretty damn easy. My 'fuck me' green eyes and styled red hair—as natural as my tits, thank you very much—have never left me in bed by myself for long, but considering Jared Turner was my last *real* relationship... yeah.

And now, a week later as I get ready to try again for New Year's, that rat is slinking out of the shadows again.

JARED T (DON'T ANSWER)

> Hey, babe. You got a date for New Year's?

> I'm in town through the third and got a night off. What do you think?

> I miss you, Tandy.

> I miss that ass. That mouth.

> Baby, please.

> Call me.

No, thanks.

Though, I have to say, like most everything else that's gone wrong in my life, Jared's whining and pleading is my fault. I used to joke that, once a guy got a taste of Tandy Lewis, he could never get over me. I tend to linger in their memories, like they're wondering if sex with me was just that good. It would explain the handful of exes that didn't take it all that well when I inevitably dumped them, though that might also be because they rarely saw it coming.

I have this thing with commitment. As in, I don't ever expect it, and I'm not about it. I could blame Jared for that, for how he promised me the world after Sierra ended things with him for good, and for how he didn't keep any of those promises. I thought I loved him. Obviously, I was wrong, but when Jared didn't even have the decency to dump me himself before he moved on to his next conquest, it messed me up.

And I know that you can't expect much from a playboy like Jared Turner. Like, once a cheater, always a cheater, right? I helped him betray Sierra, even though I honestly believed at the time that the two of them had broken up before I ever fell for any of Jared's cheesy come-on lines. It was probably just karma that Jared cheated on me with Molly May, the nineteen-year-old supermodel, while Thr33peat was in the middle of disbanding.

But it's twelve years later now, and as much as I want to believe that Jared still holds a torch for me, I know better. As though both of us are still stuck in the heyday of our teenage years, Jared is absolutely obsessed with Sierra. Between being proud that her break-out hit, 'Heart Barely Used', was written about him, and secretly aggravated that—as her alternate persona, Whiskey Rose—she became untouchably famous after they broke up, he's determined to win her back.

Sometimes it works. Gossips in our circle always start whispering whenever Jared and Sierra have another of their random hook-ups over the years, but despite the occasional invite into her bed, Sierra has never invited him back into her life, and that frustrates the hell out of him.

That makes me the fallback guy. What's worse is that, over the years, I've been desperate enough to fuck him when I had no one else. He's never come out and *said* that I'm the backup plan when Sierra's avoiding him, but when it's obvious, it's obvious—and tonight, it's *obvious*.

Of course he needs a date for New Year's. If I thought my need to get laid to compensate for my overwhelming loneliness was bad, that's nothing compared to Jared. He, at least, has some level of success. Me? I'm the most famous has-been there is these days, even if I'm trying to make something of myself.

And that does not include starting my new year full of regret. Fucking Jared Turner out of pure desperation? It might feel good in the moment, but I'll definitely regret that on January 1st.

So instead of answering him, I leave the horndog on read.

The party I got a last-minute invite to starts at nine. It's the sort of shindig that you don't show up on time to, so though it's about eight-thirty now, I was just finishing up my make-up and checking to make sure that the little black dress I bought on clearance was perfectly revealing when Jared's first text came through.

There's time to at least humor my own curiosity. Closing the messages app and flicking open my search engine, I type in 'Whiskey Rose' and wait to see that she's singing live tonight in Times Square, or that she's been named the number one pop singer by Billboard for the third year in a row, or her latest movie made billions—

Holy shit.

Sierra is *pregnant*?

<hr>

EVERYWHERE I'VE GONE THESE LAST FEW DAYS, ALL I SEE is red.

Well, red and green, but that makes sense. I've been in Manhattan since the beginning of December, headlining this nostalgia show one of the midtown clubs runs four nights a week—and twice on Saturday—to sucker in all the cash from the increased number of tourists who visit the city for the holiday season. As a former member of the hit girl group, Thr33peat, I have the prestigious position of closing out the show, singing a couple of our old hits with the help of a few backup singers.

It's New Year's Eve. It takes me longer to get across town than I want it to, but that's to be expected. The ball drops at the stroke of midnight so that all of New York can celebrate ringing in the new year. It's crawling with those same tourists, and though my home base is in central Jersey these days, I like to think of myself as a city girl at heart.

I know the tricks. I know the shortcuts. I sure as

hell know how to get to the Dorado, though I've only been here a handful of times.

Sierra has the entire floor below the penthouse. A building full of celebrities, if it wasn't for the fact that Billie Bickles—'Two' in Thr33peat, another one of my best friends, and the only one who gave me the tiniest benefit of the doubt that I wanted to hurt Sierra when I hooked up with Jared—invited me in before while Sierra was busy, I'd never have known how exclusive of an apartment building it is.

Billie is Sierra's manager these days. The two are crazy close, and Billie made it clear that she will choose Sierra's side no matter what. At the same time, she fucking *hates* Jared, and once I presented my side of the story, she at least didn't hate *me*.

Then the strangest thing happened. About six months or so ago, last summer when I was taking a break between the two cruiseship tours I'd been hired to sing on, Sierra reached out to me.

Honestly? After twelve years, I never thought she would talk to me again. I wouldn't blame her, either. Whatever my reasons were at the time, the truth is that I *did* fuck her boyfriend. When it came out that Jared hadn't quite ended things with her while he was sleeping with me, she dumped him, and I... I didn't. We stayed together until Jared moved on to the next girl, and by the time I realized how much I messed up, she refused to hear me out.

I would've done the same thing. Oh, I tried to explain—but how could I? I was wrong. I've paid the price for it a million times over now, watching Whiskey Rose soar while Tandy jumps from gig to gig, guy to guy, the entire time still carrying around the weight of what I'd done as a reckless twenty-year-old kid.

And then Sierra reached out through Billie, and though she invited me to sit down with her at her place, meet face to face in the privacy of her fancy apartment in the city, I couldn't bring myself to go.

Part of that had to do with most of the level of infamy surrounding Sierra—and not just because of her super famous persona. About two years back, some whackjob tried to go after her with a gun. Then she had a very public meltdown on her latest tour before disappearing from the public eye for a bit at the end of last year.

Since then, she's come back with a vengeance. She starred in her third movie, won all these awards, and started prep on her next album. I couldn't imagine why now, out of nowhere, she felt like we needed closure or to work things out, but I came up with excuse after excuse to avoid meeting in person.

We talked on the phone. I finally got the chance to apologize, she seemed to accept it, and though there wasn't any scuttlebutt about her having a man after another one of her crazed fans broke into her apartment, she must be a pro at hiding her private life because, right there as part of Pop News's breaking story, is a picture of a visibly pregnant Sierra.

It had to be snapped by a pap. She's walking down the street, our old head of security, Roy, right at her elbow, and it doesn't matter that she's wearing a coat to ward off the December chill. She's got a bump, and I have questions.

Is it my business? Of course not. But we were the best of friends growing up. From fifteen to twenty, we were closer than sisters. Nearly every black mark on my record—in this country and countless others—is because I did something with Sierra that Billie always ended up rescuing us from. So we had a falling out. In the last few months, it almost seemed like we were friends again.

For fuck's sake, Sierra even sent me a Christmas card to the club where I've been performing these last few weeks. Of course she was too busy to catch the hour-long performance, but a card signed by Sierra Landry—hand-signed, too, not a replication—has to count for something, right?

And now I discover she's pregnant because Jared is freaking out. She's *pregnant*, and she didn't tell me?

During the downtime on those long-ago tours, we would talk about what our future husbands and children would be like. As far as I know, Billie's most recent relationship ended badly, and she's off communing with nature or some shit to get over it. Sierra's tête-à-têtes are worldwide news nowadays, but at least I'm pretty sure she hasn't secretly gotten married.

Me? I'm perennially single, with no hope of having any kids unless my birth control fails—and I'm careful enough that that will never happen.

But Sierra... maybe it's the loneliness of the recent holiday getting to me. Maybe it's my New Year's resolution to make amends with Sierra, find a steady job, and maybe search for a real relationship instead of another fling... whatever it is, I don't head toward the party I'm supposed to be going to. Instead, I make my way to the Dorado.

I might have fallen out of the limelight over the last couple of years, but I still have connections. My face is still pretty recognizable. And, sure, I expect to be reminded of my youthful indiscretions whenever someone figures out that I'm *the* Tandy Lewis, but after talking to the night doorman and concierge at Sierra's building, none of that is necessary.

He takes one look at me, nods, and says, "Evening, Ms. Lewis. Take the elevator on the left. Go straight up. Ms. Landry has been expecting you."

She *has*?

I'm not the type to look a gift horse in the mouth. If that guy thinks Sierra's going to be pleased I'm dropping in unannounced on New Year's Eve without an express invitation, I'm not going to be the one to correct him.

Taking his advice, I tuck my clutch under my arm and press the 'up' button. Stepping inside the mirrored elevator, I fluff my hair as I make my way to the top.

The elevator deposits me in a narrow hall that leads to Sierra's front door. I form a fist, ready to knock, then remember that the man at the desk said she's waiting for me. I'm still surprised by that, but even more surprised that the famous Whiskey Rose is staying home on New Year's freaking Eve.

Grabbing the knob, I turn it. My eyebrows wing up.

The door's unlocked.

Weird. I guess, since the Dorado has a doorman and a concierge down below, Sierra doesn't worry about security. The elevator needs to be keyed-in to get to her floor, so even if one of the other residents decided to go around and check if the doors were open, they couldn't. In that case, she could leave it open if she wants—which makes it easier for me.

Letting myself into the apartment, telling myself that Sierra would expect nothing less from Tandy Lewis—who could've tried calling her but, nope, she made an unexpected appearance instead—I walk in.

"Hello?"

No answer.

My heels clack against her floor. I raise my voice. "Sierra? Billie? You guys here?"

Still nothing.

None of the lights are on. I find one switch and flip it. The room off of the hallway is a fancy living room, complete with a chaise lounge and a mantelpiece full of every sort of award an entertainer in my industry can win.

No Sierra, though.

Just in case, I step into the room. Looking around, I double-check that she's not hiding in a corner—I don't know why, it makes sense at the time—before I turn, ready to see if she's hanging out in the kitchen.

However, right as I do, something catches my attention out of the corner of my eye.

What's that?

CHAPTER 3
GRIMOIRE DU SOMBRA

TANDY

It's a book.

Now, I'm not much of a reader. Never have been. It happens. While Billie's nose was always in a book, and she nagged Sierra enough that they formed their own little two-person book club while I napped on the tour bus, I never saw the point in reading. Part of a best-selling girl group by the time I was fifteen, touring the world from sixteen to twenty before it all came crashing down... I had more than enough adventures in my real life. I didn't need to read about them.

Same thing with romance. Before Jared, I convinced myself I was in love with Corey, the bad boy of Cool Guyz. He was my first everything, and when that didn't work out, he left me easy pickings for his bandmate to scoop up.

I've been head-over-heels in love—or believed I was. I've experienced heartache. Betrayal. Hurt. None of my romances came with a happily ever after, and reading about them made me jealous of the fictional characters.

True love doesn't exist. There's infatuation and lust —I won't deny that—and sudden attraction that'll have my ankles up by my ears for a guy with a charming smile and a couple of slick lines. But romance?

Like chivalry, I'm pretty sure it's dead.

But that's okay. I don't need love to get laid, and if I'm not happy with my lot, that's what the new year is for, right? Things will get better.

Hey. At least I'm not the one knocked up, yeah?

But a book... I shouldn't be nosy. Not that it's going to *stop* me or anything. That book isn't mine, and for all I know, it's a baby name book. Maybe it was a gift from Billie to Sierra for Christmas. I could see her giving Sierra an old, rare book that was hard to get her hands on amidst plenty of other gifts.

Then again, there's no sign that anyone celebrated Christmas only just last week. And though I'd bet that Sierra and Billie have a housekeeper and a crew that would put up decorations for the famous starlet, then take them down when the holiday is over, I kind of expected there'd be *some* hint of the holiday lingering.

It's only New Year's Eve. Way I see it, we're in that weird no man's land week that separates Christmas Eve from New Year's Day. When you lose track of what day it is, and when your work schedule is fucked.

I don't have another show until January 3rd. This is my vacation, and instead of spending it at a New Year's Eve party, drinking champagne and cruising for my conquest, I'm snooping around my old friend's seemingly empty apartment.

I should've known better. Whiskey fucking Rose wouldn't be hanging around her apartment on New Year's Eve, pregnant or not. Bille, maybe, but I haven't heard from her in a while. I actually kind of thought that the only reason Sierra got into touch in the first place was because Billie needed to step back in her role as Sierra's manager and closest friend, and now Sierra, like me, was feeling a little lonely.

Yeah... I'm pretty sure I just transferred my own feelings and insecurities onto a wealthy, famous, powerful celebrity. But that book...

The more I look at it, the more I think I might've seen it before.

Setting my clutch down on the back of Sierra's maroon couch, I move until I'm standing next to the coffee table. This close, I know my strange sense of déjà vu wasn't an exaggeration.

I *have* seen this book.

Like I said, I've never been much of a reader. The truth is that I was put off of reading when I was a teen because, for almost two years consistently, I kept dreaming about one old book in particular.

Weird, huh? What kind of normal sixteen-year-old girl falls asleep and her recurring dream is searching for an old leather book that she could never, ever find? It was super frustrating, and the first time I got drunk in Amsterdam, it was because I was trying to burn the memory of the strange book out of my head.

It worked... eventually. One day, I dreamed about the book and a pair of large, featureless shadows whirling just beyond the lectern it was kept on. The next? I fantasized over Corey Hanks, his pouty lips, and his expensive emo haircut.

After Corey, there was Jared. Tucker. Coop. Marcus. Benji. Jaime... the list goes on and on, I'm sure I've forgotten a couple that came and went in the first few years after my world came crashing down, but when boy-crazy Tandy spent all her time looking for the next guy to make her feel *something*, she stopped dreaming about books.

To be honest, I forgot about it entirely—until right this very second.

I've never told anyone about my strange dreams

before. Well, no. That's not exactly true. I mentioned it once, Sierra and Billie teased me so mercilessly over it that Roy had to step in before our argument turned into a catfight, and I refused to discuss it again. Realizing the topic made me touchy—and a far better friend to me during our Thr33peat days than I ended up being to her—Sierra didn't bring it back up after that. Neither did Billie.

And yet, for some strange reason, it's *here*. Sitting in the middle of Sierra's coffee table, almost as if it's waited for close to fifteen years to find me...

Bending over slightly, I get a better look at it.

The book is *old* old. From the pitted leather cover to the yellowed pages, I can't even begin to imagine how long it's been since it was printed and bound. Ages. Unless it's some kind of prop for one of Sierra's new movies. It's possible. It could just *look* old—

I pick it up. The 'old book' smell is noticeable as I bring it close to my face, but there's something else that has my nose wrinkling and a tickle forming in the back of my throat. A sort of nasty 'rotten egg'-y smell that has me choking a little.

Weird.

Breathing through my nose until the stink is gone, I look over the closed book. No title. No author. Nothing. Flipping open the front cover, I see a list of names handwritten on the inside: *Susanna.* AMY. *Shannon. Kennedy.*

No Sierra, I notice. Hm. I wonder what that's about. The second name looks like a kid wrote it, and the other two names are smeared, so while I'm not one hundred percent what they say, I don't think I'm wrong.

I look at the next page.

Grimoire du Sombra. There's no author. No copyright year. Just a title typed in an unusual font.

Grimoire? Like a magic book? Spells?

Okay. So I'm thinking this might be a prop after all. I don't change my mind when I finally notice that there's a vivid pink bookmark poking out of the top.

Shrugging, I use my fingernail to flip the page open to the page Sierra was on, careful not to lose her bookmark or her place.

Verus Amor. Beneath the printed title at the top of the page, someone wrote beneath it in a classic script: *true love.* Considering the script matches, it could be Susanna, the first name written on the inner cover. It looks faded, too, like it was written a long time ago. Years, definitely. Decades, probably.

A second later, it sinks in, and I blink.

A true love spell?

This is a *true love* spell?

Hell, yeah. Sign me the fuck up!

A laugh escapes me. I know it can't be real. Sierra's probably practicing for her role as a lovesick, lonely woman using magic to find her true love instead of relying on online dating. It's an amazing dupe, though, so props to the, well, *prop* department, I guess.

The little details really make you second guess if a spell book could actually exist. From the names scrawled on the inner cover to the translation beneath the title, and even the added comments in the margin...

Lifting the book closer to my face, completely ignoring the fact that my last eye doctor appointment revealed I'll need reading glasses sooner or later, I see that the same doodler marked two individual typed paragraphs. Each one is written in a language unlike any I've ever seen before, but the notes are in English. Next to the top paragraph, it says 'manifest'. The second claims it's a 'promise'. There's also a drawing of a pentacle, and something about using yellow chalk and salt to create it or something... I don't know. I'm more fascinated by the idea that this could possibly be an actual true love spell.

Isn't that what prop departments do? To make it as realistic as possible, they do their research.

Now, do I believe that, if I read these two paragraphs out loud, my true love is going to walk through Sierra's apartment door, whisk me off of my feet, and carry me away to our happily ever after?

Ha. Not a chance.

But if it, I don't know, helps the right guy somehow find *me*? I wouldn't say no to that.

Can you believe it? Deep down, Tandy Lewis still is holding out hope that there might be someone out there for her. I've always figured I was just too much for one man to handle, but what if there was really someone out there for me? Who'll love me, never betray me, and want me for me?

What if I have a true love?

I don't bother with chalk. Salt? This isn't my place, and even if it was the hotel I've been renting for the run of my latest show, I rarely use the condiment. I might have a couple of those tiny packets from my take-out orders, but that's it. Enough to draw that five-point star with the circle around it? Unlikely.

Besides. Nothing's going to happen, and I begin reading the strange words even as I'm convinced of that fact.

The sounds make no sense. The syllables are harsh, and some of the words make me feel like I'd be better off gargling rocks than attempting to read them. Part of me thinks that, even if it *did* work, I'm butchering the language so badly, the spell will fail regardless.

Um. Spoiler alert.

It *doesn't.*

To my surprise, something actually does start to happen after I finish the first paragraph.

It's December in the city, where my teeth chattered all the way to the front door because my dress is so short and the temperature is so fucking cold out right now. It was warmer inside the climate-controlled apartment, but as my eyes travel to the second paragraph—the 'promise' part—it seems like the heat kicked in or something.

Sweat forms at the base of my spine, my meticulously styled hair starting to curl a little in the sudden blast of powerful warmth steaming up the room. Like when you walk past an open oven and get a face full of hot air, it slams suddenly into my back.

There's only one light on in the apartment. It's a cooler shade of white, but the living room I'm in has become awash with orange by the time I'm halfway through the second paragraph.

Then, just as quickly, the room shadows over. It's so dark, I think Sierra came in and turned off the light to catch my attention.

I spin on my heel, searching for her—

—and that's when I see a large... circle, I guess? I don't know. There's, like, this giant hole on the other side of Sierra's gaudy chaise. Dark on the edges, but full of flames in the middle, my brain goes: *fire*.

If it is a fire, it's contained. The flames lap at the edge of the massive pit hovering about two inches over the floor.

"What the—"

Something flickers at the corner of my eye. Turning slightly, I notice something strange in the shadows that have fallen over that side of Sierra's living room.

Unless I've lost my fucking mind—and considering what led me to this exact moment in time, I very easily could have—there is a... a... a *figure* standing in the middle of the shadows.

I stare, and the shadows *move*.

CHAPTER 4
I PROMISED?

TANDY

One second, the ghost of some unfamiliar figure is a black mass of shadows with very indistinct features. The next? It—*he*—solidifies into a monstrous-looking *guy*.

And I don't mean he's ugly. Even as I flinch, recoiling away from his outstretched claws, I don't think he's *ugly*. Different, definitely. His skin is a deep red color, his hair as black as ink and longer than mine as it spills in a sheet down his back. He has horns the same color as his hair, arching up and over his head. His muscles have fucking muscles, he's that ripped, and if he's anything shy of seven feet tall, I'll eat my stiletto heel.

He has ridges over his brow. Nothing covers his

chest, though my initial panicked inspection reveals that his lower half is covered in the same shadows that made up the rest of him only moments ago.

And his eyes...

His eyes are the strangest part of a strange ass monster *thing*. I don't know what he is, a demon or what, but his eyes make my stomach go queasy and my brain catch up to what I'm seeing in front of me enough for my fight or flight instinct to kick in.

He has two different colored eyes. They're both glowing brightly out of his dark face, one of them a vivid white, the other undeniably *purple*.

The monster says something to me in a surprisingly soft voice. Do I know what it is? Fuck, no. It's in that same unfamiliar language, and I'm too busy screaming inside of my head to make out anything he's telling me.

So I decide to scream out loud. That seems like the thing to do, right? Scream bloody murder so that the monster decides that I'm too much trouble to gobble up.

Because, trust me. I've been with enough guys to know when someone is imagining serving me up on a silver platter, and this monster? Whether he wants to eat me or *eat* me, I don't know what sort of hunger is crossing his features at the moment, but I avoid his outstretched hand—claws, I think again, look at those freaking two-inch-long *claws*—just in time to turn and bolt in any other direction than where he is.

Big mistake, Tandy. Big, big mistake.

Because the second I turn, I end up right in the embrace of someone as big, as solid, and as physically hot to the touch as I'm betting the other monster is.

His arms close around me for a fleeting second. Just then, I feel safe, but it lasts half as long as that second. Safe? How can I be safe when there are two of them?

Holy shit, Tandy, there are *two* of them.

I back up, nearly falling thanks to my three-inch heels, and I spin, searching from one of the monsters to its—*his*—twin.

There is not a single doubt in my mind that, whoever they are... *whatever* they are... they're identical twins. Hang on... no. Not identical. While each of these two demonic-looking beasts has one purple eye, one white eye, it's the reverse on the other. Like they're mirror images, only instead of looking at their brother, they're looking at *me*.

The first monster says something else.

His twin responds.

I whimper, realizing that I brought these two here with that stupid fucking spell, and now I'm trapped between them.

One of the monsters is at my back. The other is

stalking toward me, but he's so bulky, he's basically blocking me from leaving the living room through the door that leads out to the hall. He's big, but his steps are careful, and I know without knowing how, if I make a break for it, he's quick and nimble enough to stop me.

So I don't go anywhere. I stand between them, pretending like they're t-rexes or something, and that if I don't move, they won't see me.

I wish that worked. It doesn't, of course. Just because they're speaking to each other in another language doesn't mean they're unintelligent. I don't think they are. There's intent in every move they make, and an emotion on their faces that is so similar to human desire, my knees go a little weak.

That proves to be my downfall. I stumble, and the second I do, the two of them are *right there*.

One of the big red monsters takes my right hand. The other grabs my left.

I don't know what happens next, or how to really explain it. Though there's something strangely alluring about their chiseled features, their height, their sculpted chests, and their mismatched eyes, and I've been known to be attracted to anyone with a cock and a pulse—and if they're proportionate in size, they've got to have monster dongs hidden under those shadows of theirs—this is *insane*.

I can't want to fuck a monster. Like, I have to have limits.

And yet... the moment their heated flesh touches mine, I don't scream again. I don't try to fight. I let them grab me, a rush of arousal making me just as hot as these two, and when they tug on my arms, it isn't until they're carrying me through the fiery portal that I even worry about being burned to a crisp.

I SURVIVE.

There were flames. I swear there were. But the second I'm yanked through the portal, they seem to disappear. At the very least, I'm not burned, though when I find solid ground beneath my heels again, the room is so warm, I immediately start to swelter.

I'm inside somewhere. Where? No fucking clue. It's a somewhat bare space, twice the size of my hotel room, with an empty silver-looking bathtub on one side of the room, a table made out of dark wood on another, and a huge—and I mean *huge*—bean bag-looking thing with a fur-like covering serving as a blanket taking up most of the space.

There's a window, too, and I slip out of their hold before they can increase their grip on me. I can squirm when necessary, and I've spent the last fifteen years on heels so they don't slow me down at all.

Within seconds, I'm at the window, and the only thought running through my head when I see the inky black shadows surrounding a field of red, black, and grey ash is: *oh, Tandy. I don't think you're in Kansas—er, Manhattan—anymore.*

Shit. For that matter, thanks to the strange black moon with the sliver of a gold one peeking out along the side of it, I don't think I'm even on *Earth*.

Is that what happened? I... what? Accidentally summoned a pair of demon twins who *kidnapped* me to their realm?

I don't know. I can't talk to them, either, since they clearly don't speak English. My phone is back at Sierra's place, tucked in the clutch I never had the chance to grab. I have nothing but my panties, my dress, and my heels, though even if I did snatch my phone up, what good would it do? It's not like I'll get service on a different plane of existence, and as impressive as translation apps are, could I really use one to find out what they're saying—

"Be at ease, Tandy. I am Lucian. That is my brother, Damien. Do not fear. We will not harm you."

Well, first of all, I didn't think they were going to until he made it a point to assure me that they wouldn't. Second—

"You can... you can talk? I mean, in English?"

Lucian nods. "Because of your essence, dear one. Thank you. It's clear that you don't know Sombran—"

"Sombran?" I ask, interrupting the monster and not really caring that I did. He took me here. Both of them did. The least they can do is explain where *here* is.

"Yes. We are Sombra demons. This is our world. Our home. And your room." He gestures around us. "From your essence, we know you are used to your own quarters. If there is anything you require in it, just ask."

From my... essence? Forget about this being my room. Sue me, but I'm more interested in the other thing he said.

"Essence?" I echo. "What the hell does that mean?"

If I thought he'd be put off by my blunt demand, I'm wrong. He isn't. Not even a little. Instead, he gentles his voice. "Your essence, Tandy. That which makes our mate *her*. Makes you *you*. All of your thoughts, your memories, your emotions... your experiences. Your language. Your honored my twin and me by gifting us your essence."

I did no such thing. "Uh, no."

Lucian nods. "But yes. When we took your arm and brought you to our home. To *your* home. You, dear one, recognized us instinctively as your males and gave us your essence. And now, until you take ours in return, we speak in your human language instead of our demon tongue."

Demon... he said something like that before? And maybe I'm trying too hard to look past this idea that these two *demons* know everything about me sall of a sudden, like they got a Tandy download without me knowing how to cut off the connection, but I'm ready to get back to *that* topic.

"Demons?" I repeat. Look at that. I guess my initial reaction was right, if that counts for anything. They are demon twins!

"We are the doppelseers," he continues.

And... he's lost me again. Though, to be fair, I'm not sure he ever found me.

"The what? Hold on. Let's backtrack to you guys being *demons*—"

"We, dear one, are your mates."

Okay. That one renders me speechless for a second.

I can only think of a few reasons why he would use that word, and considering I doubt the UK or Australia has two moons like this place does, I highly doubt he means 'mate' like 'buddy'.

"Mates? Like... 'fucking' mates? 'Banging' mates?" I lift my hands. With my left, I form a circle with my thumb and pointer finger. With my right, the pointer finger stays extended. I poke the hole I made. "Mates, like you want to do this to me?"

Lucian's eyes light up. As the glow brightens, the purple looks paler, closer to the strange white color of his other eye. "Are you prepared to take us now? We can claim you each first or together. How is it done with humans?" He gestures at the big-ass bean bag chair. "Would you like to mate now? Or," he adds,

smile that should terrify me instead of make me curious about how he wields those suckers when he kisses—and when he does other things with his mouth.

"You are a most interesting female, dear one," says Lucian. "The gods have blessed us with the perfect mate."

Mate again. "I'm not your mate—"

"You are."

For the first time since we arrived in this room, Damien speaks up.

There's something about his voice. His tone. It's musical, and much softer than you'd expect from a demon his size. It's oddly alluring, too, and I have no choice but to look over at him—and, yup, there goes the shivers running up and down my spine again.

"No," I say firmly. He knows English now, too. He knows exactly what I'm saying. "I'm not."

Unlike his twin, Damien's eyes don't go bright. They dim, and for some reason, that tightens up my nervous stomach.

And then he says, "But you are. You made the mate's promise. After you manifested us in your world with the first part of the matefinder spell, calling your males to you, you vowed to be our mate. You gave us your essence. You are *ours*. We have *seen* it."

Huh?

I *am*?

No. There has to be a mistake. I didn't promise these two monster guys anything—

Oh.

Oh.

The first part of the spell I read... it said 'manifest' in the column, didn't it? *Verus amor*... how much do you want to bet that's the matefinder spell the scowling demon dude just mentioned. And the second paragraph... didn't it say 'promise'?

Welp, I obviously manifested two hulking, surprisingly attractive demons into Sierra's apartment before they brought me to their world.

Who's to say I didn't do exactly what Damien said and promise to be their mate without having any clue what I was doing?

Happy fucking New Year, Tandy.

Pity I didn't put summon a pair of demon twins to *marry* onto my New Year's resolution list.

CHAPTER 5
HOPE

LUCIAN

In Sombra, if you are born with the tell-tale purple eyes, you know that you are fated to be a mage. It is the mark of magic, telling our fellow demons that we have mystical powers that extend far past what they can do with their shadows.

I had them. Damien didn't.

But I corrected that. Even as a newborn spawn, I saw that our twin bond was something to treasure. I love my brother. As a mature male, I'd do the same thing I did when I was young: sending half of my essence down our bond so that he would be a demon instead of demonic. That meant he had half of my powers as well, including sight and the ability to conjure.

Of course, with each of us having only half of our essence, our abilities manifested in different ways. It's most obvious in how we serve as seers. I actually have the sight while Damien? He reads others in a way I've always been in awe of.

The same is true of our mage talent. Like with my visions, I can *see* what I want and make it a reality. Damien's powers rely on items reacting to his emotions. Like how, when he can't contain his frustration at our long wait, he would roar and the villages surrounding our home would tremble. Or how the loneliness he attempts to hide—not from me, though, because I feel it, too—would summon the essence-less creatures that lurk in the depths of the shadows to him.

As though they feel kinship with my twin, they follow him wherever he goes.

But we are the doppelseers. Though we're such different visionaries, together we became the most well-respected and revered seers in Sombran history. The same is true of our magic. Combined, we can accomplish anything.

Take our home. We built it ourselves, with magic and with our claws. But when the creatures would come and sit outside the back of it, stirring around the edge of Sombra's shadows, wordlessly inviting Damien to join them... we enchanted it. Now it moves wherever we wish, protected from all those we'd rather hide from.

Over time, we've journeyed far and wide over Sombra, visiting villages and larger demon cities, speaking our visions and earning a reputation that endures to this age.

Inside the cabin, we are its masters. With a wave of my hand, plus Damien's will, we can build rooms, add floors, summon steaming water from the ashfields for our baths, even create furniture. Food is easy enough. So long as we're near a village full of demons, we can conjure it from one of the local hunters, bakers, and growers who perform miracles of their own, creating fruits and grains out of the ash, little rain, and a few seeds. They're more than happy to share with the doppelseers, especially when we give our prophecies and visions away in exchange for their hospitality.

It works well for us. We've existed this way for nearly three millennia.

Now it's been a single moon that we've had our mate with us, and already I feel as if we've always basked in her beauty.

Tandy is *glorious*. I finally understand why the color red has haunted my twin and me all these years. As a Sombran, my skin is red. I've never seen another creature with hair the same color—until Tandy. It frames her oddly pale face and her strangely dim eyes, but I know those are human features. Like her rounded ears and flat, ridge-free brow. We had seen and met other humans before, so we were prepared for the differences in our mate.

Prepared for them, and immediately aroused by them.

The moment she called Damien and I into her quarters, using the matefinder spell to open a portal and bring us to her, my cock immediately knew that she was ours. It twitched and hardened beneath my shadow coverings; knowing that humans are more... delicate in these matters, we'd agreed to conceal any sign of how badly we ached to claim her before she understood that the gods had given her to my brother and me.

I believe she does now.

That's because of me. Damien refused to explain any more than he already had after reminding Tandy of her mate's promise. Hurt by the way she initially rejected him after he approached her in the human realm—though she turned from me, too—my twin has decided to let me take the lead on handling our female until she accepts that she is ours.

She *must*.

Tandy allowed us to take her hands after we told her in Sombran that she was our one true mate. Even before we'd finished materializing in the human world, she was already giving us the mate's promise. She didn't guard her essence as we held onto her during the quick trip back to Sombra, allowing it to fill both Damien and I.

Now it is *ours*.

And so is this stunning little mortal.

I tried to tell her myself once we brought her to the space above us, designed specifically for her in mind. The essence exchange gave us a little insight into Tandy—to our dear little one—and I could tell in an instant that she was as lonely as Damien and I. She was also in search of a male who would love her, stay true to her, and be there always.

Tandy has found them in her males, whether she realizes it yet or not.

She will. We might not have any visions in regards to her, the gods telling us in our own way that we must find a way to convince Tandy to accept our essence and our cocks without their help, but I have faith in my brother and myself. We will claim her, and we will do so before the next gold moon.

Otherwise, if the prophecy we foretold to Haures all those millennia ago comes to pass first, then all of this would've been for naught.

Time is running out. The three of us—Damien, Haures, and I—have known for more than twenty centuries that once the human world of legend mingled with Sombra, it could lead to the end of our realm as we know it.

Damien saw the prophecy first, and he explained it as this:

A child born of two worlds,
belonging in both, belonging to none,
will bring with them rain,
and the fires of Sombra will be forever done.

It took us decades to understand exactly what the prophecy meant, despite how seemingly straightforward it might appear. I had multiple visions myself, and they all end the same: a tiny half-mortal, half-demon who manifests rain in Sombra when it cries, manifests flooding when it's missing from this realm, and manifests whipping storms when it is separated from its mother.

The child itself is cloaked in shadows, similar to how the visions about my own future are; most likely because the end of Sombra affects all of us. It was clear from the start, however, that it is part human, though I could never see the identity of the parents, either. To keep the prophecy from coming true too soon, Haures put into place his first law: no contact between the human realm unless a true mate summoned their demon partner to them.

It was essential. Both Haures and my brother and I knew that we were fated to mate human females eventually. Haures would be first, Damien and I last to find them, but so long as a demon male refrained from mating his female during the gold moon, we could keep the prophecy at bay.

And then the demon artist Malphas found his mate in a human female called Shannon, and once she was expecting his spawn, the sands of time started to fall.

We are in a race against it. Haures has his mate, but while he is a bondmaster, he is no seer. If Damien and I bond our mate to us, we will finally be whole. Our powers will increase exponentially, and with that, we might finally be able to see past the prophecy in order to prevent it.

The child will be born. There is no doubting that. Any moon now, in fact, which means that we must find a way to convince Tandy to be our mate sooner than later. Though, if I'm being truthful with myself, it is not so much the fate of Sombra that has me desperate to make her ours as my own desire to finally claim our mate.

I cannot deny it, and it's all due to the bond that snapped into place when she promised herself to us, giving us the mating promise that now has me aching to hold her in my arms while taking her at the same time as Damien.

But that must wait. Human mates need to be wooed, and whenever she allows me to, I try.

Damien... well, he will. As soon as Tandy is receptive to me, she'll be receptive to him, and he can show her that he will be a good mate to her just like I vow that I shall.

Whatever it takes.

TANDY IS MADDENINGLY STUBBORN.

It has now been four moons. Four mornings. Four eves. Telling me with a defiant tilt to her head that we gave her the room so she sees no reason to leave it, she's stayed upstairs despite my repeated offers for her to explore the rest of the cabin.

I want her to like it. It is her home now, and if there's something about the space that she wants adjusted, she need only tell us and it is done.

She insists that she has everything she needs once I explained to her how she was to relieve herself. Our bathtub needs magic to summon fresh water from the hot springs and disappear it, but we also have a water tube that's of a temperature acceptable enough for her to drink. After the first night when she refused, she's eaten every meal we've prepared for her. I wove her three dresses out of shadows that mimicked the one she was wearing when she summoned us, plus feet coverings after she admitted that the ones she had on —with the points on the end that made our wee mate appear a bit taller—were causing her discomfort.

She is pleasant at times. Endearingly sassy at others. Her essence reveals that she is doing her best to make sense of her new reality.

I am a logical male. Damien is ruled by his emotions, but I see clearly, and I lay out the facts. In my way, I made it clear to Tandy that she is ours. She gave us the mate's promise. We have no intention of returning her to her human realm, no matter how she pleads sweetly or uses harsh human language that nearly singes my pointed ears.

She will understand. I am a logical male, and a good one, but most of all, I am determined.

I need Tandy. I need her affection. Her smiles. Her heart.

Her cunt.

If I do? Damien needs it double. Every day she is here, he withdraws further, though he insists that he is just biding his time until Tandy is ready to accept that we are her males.

She stays upstairs in her quarters. We've conjured a small room below that we share so as not to intrude on her space until she welcomes us into it. Currently, Damien is sitting at the table, tapping his claw against a bottle of demon wine that was given to us as a gift from a grateful clanleader.

"You spent hours with Tandy this morning," he says softly, and while there is no jealousy in his tone —because he is never jealous of me, only of the males that flash across his consciousness now that we have Tandy's essence—I can't help but experience guilt regardless that I spend most of the time wooing Tandy while Damien lurks in the shadows downstairs. It's his choice, and yet... "Has anything changed, Lucian?"

I shake my head. "When I look at Tandy, I see rain."

In a fiery world like Sombra, we have only enough rain to survive. It is essential that we do. We are made of shadows. Without light, there is no shadow. With too much rain, there is no fire. If we flood...

There is no Sombra.

Damien blows out a rush of air through his nose. He jerks his head, the light from our enchanted orb reflecting off his horn. "She does not want us."

"She will," I say encouragingly.

"I wish I had your faith, brother. But she prefers human males. I see them in my head. She was quite desirable in her world, and the gods know she is what we dreamed of and more. But we are so different... why would she choose us?"

That's what Damien says. Only I know what he means: why would she choose me?

He feels so much, but it's not always pleasant.

I crouch down next to him, laying my hand on his thigh.

"You don't have to look at her past, Damien. We all have them, and we cannot fault Tandy for what she did before she knew she was fated to be our one true mate. We are the doppelseers. We look to the future."

His white eye flares. Just the white one. "I am aware. I'm sorry. I... I'm trying."

I sigh, then rise back up so that I'm standing. "I know."

Poor Damien. My twin has never been so close to losing his constant battle with letting go of his tenuous hold of our essence, releasing it completely so he can go fully demonic. I thought having Tandy near would help him, but not while he refuses to woo her himself.

But he hungers. I know he does.

I want my mate desperately, but Damien... he *needs* her.

And with time slipping quickly through our claws, I suddenly understand that we will never have the chance to claim Tandy fully before the half-demon, half-human spawn is born if Damien doesn't treat her like she is his mate.

"Go to her."

"What?"

"You must talk to her, Damien," I tell him firmly. "You haven't attempted to learn our mate. Get to know our dear one."

"I do." Damien taps his temple with his claw. "I have her essence, Lucian. I know everything about her." He drops his hand to his heart. "I sense her every movement. Her emotions. Her thoughts. I know it all."

"So why won't you tend to her? She needs to know you, too, brother."

He's quiet for a moment before he admits, "I know how badly she wanted to leave before, and how she seems to be more comfortable with the idea of staying the more you talk to her. I won't risk your chance of having a mate at last by frightening her again."

My forehead furrows as I look at Damien. "You mean *our* mate."

"Of course," Damien answers quickly. "But that doesn't change what I said. You're making headway with her, Lucian. You go."

No.

"She is not my mate," I tell him. "She is ours." Waving my hand, I summon a tray that comes with fresh-baked bread and cubes of cheese. "Here. Tandy hasn't eaten in a while. Take this up. Share this small meal. Spend time with her."

"Lucian—"

"Now." I put as much power into that one word as I can. I'm sure my purple eye is flaring now, but though I usually let Damien do what is best for him, in this, I must choose what that is for my twin. Though my guilt from earlier only increases, I do add a gentled, "Please."

Again, he's quiet for a moment as though deciding his next move. Then, with a short nod, Damien pushes up from his seat at the table.

He holds out his hand, wordlessly taking the tray. I give it to him, and after another moment's hesitation, he snatches the bottle of demon wine from the table.

Damien adds it to the tray, then stalks out of the room without a backward look at me.

I take his seat and exhale roughly.

My twin is right. I have been making headway with Tandy. Only before I came down here, I had a vision of her clinging tightly to a demon male in his shadows, her head thrown back in ecstasy as he held her to him, mating her with wild abandon. It was so fleeting, I couldn't tell if it was Damien or me, but the fact that I had a vision including Tandy at all gives me hope.

Hope that we can change the prophecy.

Hope that we can save Sombra.

Hope that she can save Damien.

And, most importantly, hope that—after so many centuries of plotting—we'll have the one thing we've ever wanted: *her*.

CHAPTER 6
JUST A KISS

TANDY

I don't know why I thought that, if I played along nicely, did what they wanted—within reason— the demons would decide that they'd troubled me long enough and send me back on my way to New York.

By the third day that I'm stuck in this room, I have to admit that they weren't kidding when they insisted that I was their one true mate, and that I'm supposed to stay with them forever.

Part of me reacts the same way I did when I saw the 'true love' spell in that old book. Like, sign me the fuck up, right? Two massive, ripped demons who look at me as if they've never seen anyone hotter... who tend to my every whim even as they take me as their captive... who promise me forever, and since Lucian insists they're immortal, they *mean* it... like, why would I refuse?

They're offering me a place to stay with no rent, I don't have to work, they feed me surprisingly tasty meals, and once I made it clear that they can't expect pussy right off the bat for the deal, Lucian vows that they will leave me to this room while bunking together down below. Only if I let them in will they enter, and he's held to his word ever since.

Part of me wants to go all in... but the part that has spent almost twenty years in the public eye—both good and bad—has learned a very valuable lesson: when something seems too good to be true, it usually is.

I haven't found a downside yet. That's probably why, after my first demands to be brought back to the city went purposely—and, admittedly, apologetically—ignored, I stopped pushing as hard for them to create one of those fiery portal things.

I mean, it's been four days at this point. I've gotta be fired by now. I missed a whole bunch of shows without calling out so there goes that contract and my rep. So, yeah, even if I went back... where would I stay? What happened to all my stuff so far? Will the hotel trash it? When no one is paying for my room, probably.

Great.

My clutch has gotta be in Sierra's apartment still. She'll know it's mine because of my phone and my ID, but will she ever figure out what happened to me? I mean, she had the book in her apartment... does she know about demons?

Or am I the only lucky chick whose true love turned out to be a pair of demon twins who insist that I belong to both of them?

How do they know that I do for sure? Surprise, surprise: these guys are, like, psychics. *Visionaries.* They see things about the past and the future, and Lucian assures me they were waiting for me long before I picked up that book in Sierra's place and used the first part of the spell to summon them to me.

I'll say one thing: it's kind of hard to convince them they got the wrong chick when they show you a chalk drawing of your face that was sketched before you met...

So I'm here. I'm not going anywhere. Fighting the situation seemed pointless to me so, over the last couple of days, I've gotten to know them. I had no choice, really. They brought me here, and though they're giving me space, if I want to eat, I have to let them into 'my' new room.

They're actually really sweet. Well. *Lucian* is. Though his twin made it a point to tell me I'm theirs, I haven't seen Damien since. Lucian assures me that his brother regrets his outburst and simply wants me to feel comfortable around them.

He's working double-time to make up for his

broody twin. Once I accepted that this was real, that this was happening, he made an effort to connect with me and, well, I let him. Just because he instinctively knows everything about me because they stole my 'essence'—which, if I understand correctly, is kind of like my *soul*—he wants to make an effort to get to know me the human way.

So we talk. I tell him about my life, glossing over the worst parts of it. He tells me about this demon realm I've found myself in and what exactly it means to be a demon's mate.

There are a bunch of perks, I'll tell you that. Some minor annoyances, too, the biggest being that I've grown up in a world that is ruled by technology. Sombra? It's basically run on magic. And while I appreciate never running out of hot water or how their fancy toilets make cleaning them obsolete so long as I don't think about where the waste goes, I miss my phone. My computer. My television.

So without anything to distract me—and when Lucian can't be around to occupy me—I've been sleeping. A lot.

Am I enjoying the rest? Not at all. I keep having these weird dreams. You'd think I'd want to stay up to avoid them, but nope, I keep falling asleep, and I keep on dreaming—and they're as vivid now as my weirdo dreams used to be.

When I was a teenager, I dreamed about that book

I found in Sierra's apartment all the freaking time. After Lucian sat with me and explained just what a 'doppelseer' means—that he and his broody, quiet brother are the only demon twins in Sombra *and* they have the ability to see the future—I've begun to wonder a little if I share a bit of their gift.

It's not just how I knew about the book, either. From the moment the demon twins grabbed me, I keep getting these inexplicable flashes of them doing all kinds of things to me. Some of them are as sweet as Lucian himself: massaging my back, serving me breakfast in that giant bean bag chair I've turned into my bed, combing my hair with their claws, and sitting together outside in a pile of surprisingly soft ash while watching flames flicker against the deep black shadows.

But, because I'm Tandy freaking Lewis, the dreams —*fantasies*—inevitably turn x-rated. I fantasize about doing everything with these guys. Sleeping with them, both separately and together. Going down on one while the other takes me from behind. Gripping one of the male's horns while he feasts on my pussy, his twin jacking off and coming all over my bare tits. Like, I've invented my own monster romance porno in my head, and I have to keep double-checking with Lucian that he can't read my mind.

Oh, no. He can tell by my 'essence' how I'm doing. He has access to my memories and my emotions, and with a nose that's really super fucking impressive, he can always tell when I'm turned on. After I made it clear that I'm not about to jump on his dick, he's been careful not to mention my need, but every time his nostrils flare and he breathes in deep... I know that he knows that I want him.

Because, fuck it, I *do*. I can't help it. The visions are definitely affecting me, and the only reason I've held off as long as I have is because I can't tell if they are *my* fantasies or if the demon can put *his* into my head.

I asked him. I've got no shame. I never have. So I asked him if he can plant those psychic visions he gets into someone else's mind, and while he admits that it's possible to share them under the right circumstances, he swears that he hasn't with me. Not until I have his essence will he attempt to try that with a human, and since he can only share his essence with me when Damien does—because of this twin bond thing they share—and Damien is avoiding me, that obviously hasn't happened yet.

Not like I *want* it to. It's hard enough to keep from reacting to this nearly irresistible pull tugging me toward Lucian—and, damn it, his twin, too—without being able to tell myself how much he wants me at any given moment. When he uses the strange woven shadows that act like leather here to hide his hard-on, I can't gauge his arousal by the obvious bulge. Still, the way he looks at me... yeah. He's down for sex.

And after another one of those x-rated dreams I just woke up from, I'm feeling a little needy myself.

The strangest part about them is that I can't tell which demon is which while I'm in the middle of the vision. Lucian and Damien are almost completely identical, except for one difference: the way their mismatched eyes are the mirror version of their brother. I've learned that Damien has the left purple eye, Lucian has the right purple eye, but in my dreams? They always duck their heads so I don't know who is who.

But when all three of us are together, I have no doubt that, even if he *is* avoiding me, Damien wants to fuck me as badly as his twin does.

Am I broken? I might be. Because as much as I can't help but be drawn to Lucian, there's something about his brother that has caught my attention. Like, he's keeping his distance, and that only makes me want him more...

Yup. I've gotta be broken.

And I tell myself that even as I start to slip my hand up my dress...

I'm so fucking horny. Leaving those dreams has me crawling with need, and though odds are that—with their sight, and with their ability to read me because of my essence—they know whenever I'm masturbating, I could give a shit.

I need to get off, and I need to get off now.

Too bad one of the demons has another idea.

Rap, tap, tap.

"Tandy? I've brought you your meal."

That lyrical yet enticing voice... *Damien.*

Pulling my hand out of my dress, I use my palm to fluff my hair, careful not to get any of the slick on my fingers in the strands. Scrabbling to my feet, I tug down the shadow dress Lucian wove for me after I complained about being stuck in my New Year's Eve cocktail dress for two full days. It's a near dupe, though it's surprisingly more comfortable even without panties or a bra.

I don't know why I didn't ask for them. Lucian made three dresses for me, but when he asked if I needed anything else to be happy here, all I wanted was a light blanket to cover me as I slept. It was only after he went back downstairs that I realized under-clothes might've been a good idea—but maybe not when I've spent the last day and a half trying to figure out how I can get one of them to fuck me without promising them any more than I already have.

I thought Lucian would be the lucky guy, but if Damien is, ahem, *up* to it...

I lean back in the bean bag chair, crossing my legs neatly at the ankle. "Come in."

I was right. It is Damien, and the second he walks into the room, his nostrils flare notably. Breathing in deep, the tray he's holding in his hands shaking slightly, he murmurs, "If ever there was a cunt that smelled as sweet, it would belong to you."

My pussy clenches at the heated way he says that. I wasn't sure if he would pick up on it. Turns out that not only did he notice my arousal immediately, but the Damien who barked at me the other night has seemed to have been replaced by this... this... *Romeo.*

And I *like* it.

With a slight inviting smile, I say, "I guess your nose is as good as your brother's."

He sets down the tray on my table. "Like Lucian, I am one of the doppelseers. I can read you. See your future, know your past... but I am also a Sombra male. You are a female in need. I can scent you anywhere in this cabin, feel your need anywhere in this realm. It calls to me, Tandy."

I raise my eyebrows at him, my heart rate picking up as I slowly push off of the bean bag chair. "And you're here. What happened, Damien? You finally answer the call?"

His hungry gaze darts away from me—but I know what I saw even as he tells me, "Lucian wanted me to bring you something to nourish you. I have bread. Cheese. There will be meat with your late supper. For now, though, I have brought you some demon wine."

I chuckle. "Trying to get me drunk?"

His brow furrows. "I thought you might prefer it to

water. I've seen you drink human wine. You seem to like the taste."

Too much sometimes, and that ends up getting me in trouble. But here in Sombra... how much trouble can I get into when I have two big, strong demon mates looking out for me?

The reminder that he knows everything about me because of some weird demon trick rattles me. What exactly does he see? I get the feeling that he's the more judgmental twin, and while there are a lot of things I'm proud of in my life, there are plenty that I'm *not*.

But if they know everything... well, fuck it. I might as well own it.

There are two things that Tandy Lewis can do exceptionally well: I can sing, and I can fuck. These two guys don't seem like they're big girly pop fans, but if they want sex as much as I do...

I pad over to him in my bare feet. He watches me warily, almost like he's the prey and I'm the predator. Maybe I am. I definitely feel like I'm on the prowl, and before he can slip out of my reach, I take a deep breath and lay my palms over his bare chest.

Like Lucian, Damien is in his solid, red-skinned form. He has shadows woven from hip height down, but no shirt. His skin is so hot, he almost burns my palms... but it feels good, too. Like curling up under a heated blanket during winter, having this big body pressing down on me will probably be amazing.

But that's later. For now? I go up on my tiptoes and, at the same time, move my hands to his shoulders. I tug down on him, and though he looks confused, Damien squats enough that I can press my lips against his.

It was a kiss. A simple kiss. If they want to fuck me, I figure this is the best way to start.

But Damien?

He doesn't kiss me back.

Instead, he waits until I feel stupid trying to coax him to open his lips any longer and pull away from him before he eases my hands off of his shoulders. His expression closes off as he backs away.

For a second, I think he's about to leave without a word, but when he does speak, it only twists the knife of rejection to make sure that it really fucking hurts.

"Lucian will bring up your supper," he mutters, and then he's gone, closing the door firmly closed behind him.

I stare at them for a few moments, then wipe my mouth with the back of my hand. That was totally my mistake. I got it all wrong, and now I know better. Lucian wants me. His twin obviously doesn't, and I'll have to remember that.

Stalking over to the tray he brought up to me, I zero in on the wine bottle.

"Happy New Year, Tandy," I say, grabbing the bottle by the neck.

In Sombra or in New York, it looks like this year might be just like the last few after all.

"Tandy?" Another knock. "Are you awake?"

I almost tell him to go away. The bread and cheese from before have barely been touched; rejection has always managed to turn my stomach and earlier today was no different. On the plus side, since I couldn't eat, I thought better about drinking that demon wine after all because, trust me, drinking on an empty stomach is no good for Tandy.

Instead, I curled up on the bean bag chair, feeling like a fucking idiot for making a move on Damien.

But that's not Damien out there, and as if his twin thinks I can't tell their voices apart yet, he tells me, "Dear one, it is I. Lucian."

I'd been expecting this. Not only because Damien made that parting shot about Lucian bringing me up dinner later, but because the nice twin can never stay away from me for too long.

Add in my shitty mood, and if they really can sense my emotions, he'd have no choice but to check on me.

I'd been expecting this, and though I'd run the scenario through my head countless times since Damien left the room, about how I would confront Lucian, about how I would ask him what the hell his twin's problem is, about how I would tell him that I need to know precisely what they expect from me... I don't do any of that.

Instead, as though I can't help myself, I'm already back on my feet by the time Lucian pushes the door inward.

The first thing I notice is that his hands are empty. I guess he decided to come talk to me without using supper as an excuse. Without the tray, he has a reason to come back up here later, and you know what?

I don't care.

His hands are empty, and before he can push me away like Damien did, I do the same thing I did earlier: I brace myself on Lucian's shoulders, shove down until he gets the hint, go up on my toes, and kiss him.

And Lucian?

Though it's obvious he's inexperienced and doesn't quite know what he's doing, this twin kisses me back.

A sense of triumph rushes through me as I enjoy the sensation of his tongue in my mouth. I probably feel like licking an ice cube to him, considering how different our body temps are, but Lucian mentioned once in passing that, as soon as our bond is finalized, we'll match.

I'll miss the sensation that I'm tonguing fire, so for as long as I can, I enjoy it.

I do have to breathe, though, and maybe immortal

demons don't because I end up having to break the kiss first.

I curl my fingers into his chest, though, and pant softly while keeping the connection. "Thanks," I whisper. "I needed that."

His eyes are impossibly bright. "I have long wondered what it would be like to kiss our mate once I discovered that was something that was done. For you to use your tongue against mine... I thank *you*, dear one."

But then his mismatched gaze flickers over to the table. To my barely touched tray—and to the bottle of untouched demon wine.

Lucian frowns. "Tandy? How much demon wine did you drink?"

Oh, sweet, sweet Lucian. "If you're asking me if I only kissed you because I'm drunk, don't worry about it. I didn't touch a drop. Maybe later, I might, but for now... I'm perfectly sober. I kissed you because I wanted to."

Just like I wanted to kiss Damien...

Did his twin tell him about what happened? I want to know, but I can't bring myself to ask. Instead, swallowing the slight lump in my throat, I ask Lucian, "Did you want me to kiss you?"

To my delight, the big demon's body shudders. "Yes," he grates out, voice gone raspy. "I told you, Tandy. I've dreamed of kissing our mate for so many lonely nights. To know your taste... it would be the greatest gift you give your males."

I tilt my chin up, excitement making me bold. Does that mean he wants another kiss? "Okay. Your turn. Go right ahead."

He hesitates, voice dropping low as he whispers, "Are you sure?"

I shrug. I don't see what the big deal is. I kissed him. If he wants to kiss me, yeah... I'd like that. "I think I can handle a kiss from you, Lucian."

The air in the room grows impossibly warmer, or maybe that's just due to my heating up as he looks at me before he makes his move.

I expect Lucian to lower his body again so that I'm within his reach. I part my lips... only to squeal when, suddenly, he grips me by my waist, lifting me up easily before hooking my legs over his shoulders.

It happens so quickly, all I can do is screech, "What are you doing?"

"What you told me I could, dear one. I'm giving our mate a kiss."

I giggle. "I know you're, like, a million feet tall and all, but even you might have a hard time kissing me while you have my legs thrown over your shoulders."

Holding me with one possessive hand, Lucian waves the other. I'm not entirely sure what the gesture means until he reaches behind me with it once he's done and the heat of his palm nearly sears my ass.

My *bare* ass.

"Lucian?" My voice is husky, yet trembling with undeniable lust. "Where are my clothes?"

"They are woven from my shadows. I can create them just like I can vanish them."

It's my turn to shudder out a breath. "But I thought you wanted to kiss me?"

"Oh, I do." The big demon lays his palms possessively on both of my ass cheeks, pushing me gently so that my pussy is brushing up against his mouth. He blows out a rush of hot air and I *squeal.* "I am going to kiss your cunt."

"You... you are?"

"If it would please you, Tandy. I would very much like to see what you taste like."

Well, when he puts it so nicely...

I grab his horns like they're a set of handlebars. Then, holding on for dear life, I use the heel of my foot to nudge his hard, muscular back.

"Well?" I ask. "What are you waiting for?"

CHAPTER 7
JEALOUSY

DAMIEN

Sometimes I wonder, should Lucian release me and I finally go fully demonic, if I would simply stop *feeling* then.

I always have. I feel love and gratitude for Lucian, desire for my mate, and pride that we are the most revered demons in Sombra apart from Haures. I feel remorse that Lucian can't use the magic that is his birthright, and appreciation for the way Haures rules Sombra, leaving us to guide him from the shadows.

I don't see the way my brother does. Not when it comes to our visions. That is his gift. He was the twin born with the magic power and the mage's purple eyes. I was the spare, without any essence or a reason to survive. I should've been left to the shadows, and I would've been if—even as a newborn spawn—my twin didn't instinctively share his essence with me through our twin bond.

For nearly three millennia, I've tried to convince him to take it back. I don't want to end my existence, but if it meant Lucian would have a better one? I'd sever our twin bond in an instant, giving him all of the essence that we shared.

I don't see—I *feel*. I sense things that are going to happen, and I explain them only using the way I experience them. I'm not like Lucian or most other seers. They open their minds' eyes and see. I can't, but between the two of us combining our unique abilities, we've become the most well-regarded visionaries in Sombra.

We are the doppelseers.

We are twins.

We share. Our essence. Our abilities. Our home... and our mate.

I always knew we would. Like Lucian, I looked forward to taking our female and making her ours. Even up until the moment that the red I sensed became *Tandy*, I was prepared to pleasure her alongside my brother.

But then I saw how much she was drawn to Lucian. How she flinched away from me, finding solace in his embrace before she recognized that he was my twin. Something shifted at that moment, and I could tell— I just *knew*—that, once again, I was taking something from Lucian that should belong to only him.

Tandy and Lucian deserve one another. He'll keep her safe and loved, and she'll make it so that he isn't alone...

Sombra demons only have essence to give to one mate for a reason. The bond stretches between a male and a female, not a female and two male twins with barely enough essence between *them*. Tandy is destined for Lucian. He doesn't see it yet, but I know.

She will choose. And though she laid her hands on me, placing her lips against mine, I know that when she does choose... she will not choose me.

I accept that. I don't know if Lucian will, but he is as helpless to ignore the pull of a mate bond as any other Sombra demon.

I can. I must. I feel so much, and I've learned to quiet the emotions when I can. Otherwise, I would take off into the shadows, letting the darkness silence them completely for me.

If I did, I would be demonic. I know that as well. I accept that, too. I don't want to lose my brother, but it would be selfish to take what I want when Lucian deserves his one true mate far more than I do.

He's upstairs with her now. Through our twin bond, I can sense him prowling carefully around Tandy, getting close without spooking her. As if he could. Her essence has taken root inside of both of us;

though it doesn't replace what Lucian provides for me, I have it, and I know everything about our female.

Which is why I'm sure that she will be *Lucian's* female.

I want her. I'd be lying if I tried to claim I didn't, and when she pressed her lips to mine, the intensity with which I wanted to hoist her up, pet her cunt, and thrust my cock up inside of her so that we would never be separated *terrified* me.

I am one of the doppelseers. I fear nothing—except for a red-haired female whose human magic might be powerful enough to heal me, or to shatter me.

Tandy would've welcomed me. She gave us her essence while we kept ours, so it shouldn't be the mate sickness pushing her to take us the way we ache to take her. I know better than to blame my own need for her on being sick myself. The mate sickness doesn't come on that quickly for us demons. No. My desire to claim Tandy has everything to do with knowing she's fated to be mine...

But she's also meant to be Lucian's. And if Tandy needs a male to pleasure her, it should be him.

I will live vicariously through my brother. Our twin bond is unique. No one else in Sombra has one so I can't say for sure why it works how it does, but unless we close each other off, I know what he's feeling. Obviously. That is what Damien does, even when he'd rather not.

I can't *not* feel.

Right now? I feel *jealous*.

Of Lucian? I've never been jealous of Lucian. He is the good twin. I am the mistake. And, yet, I'm grateful that he shares himself with me. I would begrudge him nothing. When he went to check on Tandy and their conversation turns into him tasting our mate's delicious cunt, I get to experience it so vividly, I swear I also taste the deliciousness of her musk on my lips.

It affects me so much that, the moment he first swipes his tongue through her cunt, gathering the moisture and swallowing it as if it is the finest demon wine, I want him to do it again. I send the demand through our twin bond, letting him know that I'm with them even if I can't bring myself to actually *join* them, and when I order Lucian to mate her with his tongue, he does—and I nearly explode.

We have never mated a female before. The doppelseers have never been sexual creatures, though in our earlier centuries, we would sit and plot and rub our cocks in unison as we imagined what our future mate would be like. We never stroked each other—the only time our cocks will touch is when we're claiming our mate together—but finding pleasure with my twin is like finding it with myself.

I am Lucian.

He is me.

We are the doppelseers, and as soon as we first

sensed our female would be a legendary mortal, we made the conscious decision never to partake in casual mating with any demoness we couldn't share our essence with.

Our cocks were made for Tandy. I can't give her mine, but as Lucian uses his shadowy claw to explore her cunt at the same time as he nibbles her most intimate area with his fangs, I disappear the shadows that are acting as my coverings.

My cock is ready to mate. Hard and throbbing, I jolt in place when my fist squeezes the tip. It wants to find Tandy's cunt and claim it, but since Lucian is currently pleasuring her while hoping he can do the exact same thing, I keep my feet planted on the floor below Tandy's quarters as I start to buck my hips.

Closing my eyes, I tighten my grip, imagining that I have her under me though I remain standing, and that the moans whispering from the second floor down to me aren't solely made for Lucian. For the moment, at least, I can pretend they're *mine*.

My solid hand stutters over my length. A frisson of pleasure mixed with pain has me gritting my teeth, fangs biting down past my bottom lip so that I don't howl and disturb them.

Lifting my hand to my mouth, I lick it, then grab my cock again. The friction eases, but I can't help but think what it would be like to have Tandy's mouth on me the same way that Lucian's mouth is currently on *her*.

Is that done? In Sombra, most mated demons don't talk about what they do in the shadows with their demonesses. It's possible that someone like Apollyon of Nuit might take Lilith by one of her dainty horns, guide her to her knees, and slip his cock between her fangs. I know that my instincts all but rage at me to get my mouth on Tandy's cunt, or to get my cock inside her any way it can—including *her* mouth—no matter how it is done.

If she offered now, would I succumb to my temptations? I'd be good. I'd be careful. She is a wee thing. I am more than two heads higher than she is. I might have to kneel myself to feed Tandy my cock, or she'd have to stay standing to clutch my hips, but if my cock was too big for her wee human mouth, I could fix that—

Suddenly, I have an image of Tandy doing just what I'm thinking of. My beautiful female on her knees, all that lovely red hair tossed over her shoulder as she takes a cock in her hand. Its tip is bulbous and red, though not as deep a color as would belong to a Sombran male or so thick that she struggles to wrap her lips around the head, taking the first few inches past her teeth.

I see it as if *I* am Tandy, and for a moment, I wonder why now—now of all moments—my visions are as clear as Lucian's. Then it hits me: I'm not seeing a vision of the future. This is a glimpse of the past.

Of *Tandy*'s past.

She is mortal. Over the past few decades, my twin and I have discussed what mating a human female would be like. Haures took his duchess more than thirty human years ago, and though he is also close-lipped about what *they* do in the shadows, he made one thing very clear: humans are different from demons in many ways, especially when it comes to mating.

A demon's life is both limitless and endless. When the mate we choose will be ours for the rest of our existence, it is worth waiting as long as it takes to find that one true mate the gods have given us. Humans don't have one mate. They have plenty, and only if they offer themselves to a demon with the mate's promise will they form a mate bond.

I have never known a female before Tandy. Lucian, neither. But Tandy... Haures warned us that we might not be her first lover, only that we must be satisfied to be the last.

I didn't care if she was claimed by another male. Once she called Lucian and me to her, she was ours. We would be her future, but I don't have enough essence of my own to keep from seeing her past.

Because that is what just happened. I see a male that used to hold Tandy's heart, her essence revealing that she often used her mouth on him the same way I hoped she might use it on me someday.

I understand my jealousy now. I am not jealous of my twin.

I am jealous of... of...

Jared Turner.

His name is Jared Turner.

A worthless human male who held Tandy's heart in his hand, then *crushed* it.

This is not the first time I've seen that male's face, though I've not seen our mate pleasuring him before now. Still, he's been in *her* mind. In her thoughts. Her emotions. From the moment I first took Tandy's essence inside of me, this one fair-haired, pale-skinned, scrawny human male has haunted me like an impossible specter or a phantom shade. I didn't under-stand why then, and to preserve the little bit of sanity I have remaining, I didn't pursue it.

Lucian told me the same thing that Haures did: that Tandy will have a past of her own, but that shouldn't affect our future. And yet, as my twin finally crossed the chasm between us and found a way to make Tandy his at last, I can't help but stew over this one male.

A snake, I remember. Dagon's mate inferred that our Tandy was less than honorable—and I'm still offended about that to this day, despite her aid in helping us bring Tandy to Sombra—but, to me, our female is *perfect*.

This Jared creature? He is no better than a ground-crawler.

What makes matters so much worse is that Tandy... her feelings for this male are complex. Added to my unfortunate ability to experience everything more potently than other demons, her essence tells me that she loved him once and struggles to forget him even now.

He is not Tandy's only other lover. Suddenly aware that I'm seeing her memories, feeling her emotions, I ignore enough of them to keep myself from watching her with countless other human males. It matters not to me that they pleasured my Tandy because none of them left any profound impact on her or her essence.

None except for this *Jared*.

Lucian needs his mate. Until Tandy accepts our essence and allows him to give her the mate's promise, she can conceivably leave us. She is smart. She is resourceful. She has kin in this realm who, if she asked, would lead her back to the human world—without us.

Not even our secret alliance with Haures would allow Lucian and me to chase after Tandy to the human realm if she rejects our bond before it is finalized.

So, to convince her to stay and be Lucian's forever,

there cannot be anything tying Tandy to the human world. Up until this moment, I didn't believe there was. She was as lonely as we doppelseers are, and she yearned for a fresh start.

Her 'new year'.

How can she do that when she clings to a male from her past?

A male who *hurt* her?

Reaching through my twin bond, I see if my brother has noticed that my last thread of control when it comes to our Tandy has *snapped*. I have no essence. It is impossible for me to block him the same way as I tried to keep from seeing more about my mate than any devoted male should. I know Lucian. His will is strong, and he would never allow himself to see any other males pleasuring his mate... except for his brother.

I cannot do that, not completely, but I can make sure that Tandy is never hurt by that Jared creature again.

Lucian is distracted. I sense his desire, and his anticipation. He has finished tasting Tandy. His body is coiled, needing release, and though I didn't find completion in my fist, I know that Tandy is about to welcome Lucian into her body—and, unlike me, he has no reason to resist.

My twin will never be more distracted than he is at this moment. Just as I can sense him guiding Tandy back toward the large nest we prepared for the three of us to share, I accept I will never join them.

It's better that a male on the cusp of turning fully demonic does not.

But I'm not fully demonic *yet*. I have an ounce of essence left that I claim as mine because Lucian insists it is. That, added to what we took from Tandy, gives me the ability to re-open the portal to the human world that we took after she manifested us with the matefinder spell.

Haures will not approve. He could possibly even sentence me to the shadows regardless, and even our hidden partnership over the ages might not be enough to protect me.

I do not care. For Lucian, I'll do anything.

For Tandy, I'll do even more than that.

Including going to the human realm on my own and confronting the male who once owned her heart...

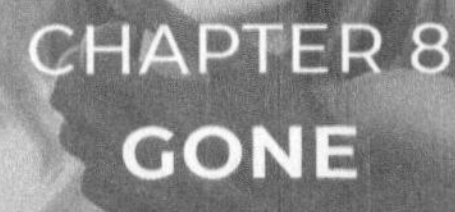

CHAPTER 8
GONE

LUCIAN

Just like kissing, I have discovered that mating is very instinctive. It's also the most pleasurable thing I've experienced in my long existence, though that's because it was our dear Tandy who allowed me to kiss her cunt with my mouth.

What made it even more memorable, too? My twin bond.

As an immature demon—older than a spawn, but not quite a mature male—I first discovered that I could find release from tugging on my cock until it gave up seed. When the visions came too quickly, or I was forced to see things I would've preferred I didn't—especially during those early days when King Yelios still ruled Sombra, he attempted to colonize other demon realms, and I saw more death and destruction than an immortal creature should—that tiny jolt of relief got me through many cycles.

Damien, too. Because, as tightly bonded as we've always been, we learned that we can sense our brother's pleasure at the same time. We're two halves of the same whole, a demon that was split into two parts before our demoness mother gave birth to us, then abandoned us to a nearby village in shame. Our adopted clanmother—long dead after her husband succumbed in the battles—raised us until our maturity, then we went off to become the doppelseers.

For millennia, I've only had my twin at my side. Stroking my cock while he was near... when we would share our future mate, why not find pleasure together whenever we could? He in his seat, me in mine, and often it was a race to see who would finish the act first.

As we grew older, our wait for our mate ever longer, the act lost its allure. My hand meant nothing when my cock knew there was a cunt destined for it. Since Tandy summoned us to her realm and we took her back with us to Sombra, I've waited with as much patience as I could muster to finally discover what it was like.

I now know that her cunt is salty yet amazingly sweet, and I hungered for it as I swiped my tongue through her folds. Even better, though I am still in Tandy's given room and Damien is down below us, I could sense him through our bond. While I pleasured our female, he took his own cock in hand, stroking it as he sent instructions to me through our bond.

He wanted me to kiss her cunt, then mate it. Knowing that my cock will someday be welcomed inside of her, my tongue found her entrance first. As a Sombra demon, I can be solid, in my shadows, or a mixture of both. Since Tandy has been with us, I've grown used to staying in my demon form so that *she* can get used to our differences, though I've purposely kept my claws as shadows when she's near so that I do not accidentally scratch her.

As she is so much shorter than me and my twin, we don't have to worry about the points of our horns goring our mate like they might if we had cause to battle another demon. I've left them solid and shiny, and I smiled into the fascinating red curls covering Tandy's cunt when she gripped one horn fearlessly and used it to steer my face where she wanted me to lick and suck next.

But when I turned my tongue to a mix of shadow and flesh after that, forming a blunt point at the end to mimic my cock before I thrust it up inside of her, Tandy tugs my horn with such strength, my nose bumps up against the tiny bump near the top of her cunt.

She screams.

I rear back, momentarily forgetting about Damien

and how he was pleasuring himself to the sensation of his twin mating our Tandy with his tongue. I clutch her behind, making sure she doesn't fall, though as tightly as she's gripping my horn, I do not think I have to worry about that.

But Tandy did scream, and as I search her face for some sign that I nicked her cunt with my fangs or inadvertently hurt her in some unknown human way, she starts slapping my shoulder with one hand while clinging to my horn with the other.

"Put me down, put me down, put me down."

I do exactly as our mate commands.

Once she's on her feet, she scurries across the room. I admit, though I'm still frantic I did something wrong while kissing her cunt, I do enjoy the sight of her breasts and her bottom bouncing. Demonesses are much slimmer in the same areas than human females, and I find I much prefer our Tandy's softness even if I have nothing to compare to it other than my sight.

To my amazement, she's not racing for the door. The opposite direction, in fact, as my wee human dives for the nest we conjured for her. It nearly swallows her whole, and the shadow blanket I wove for gets twisted around her pale ankle. She kicks it, the thin covering goes flying, and after she rolls around the nest for a moment, she's on her back.

As I stare, she scoots a little to make room for me, then lets her legs fall open, allowing me to see our naked mate completely bare and open and on display for us.

No.

For *me*.

Damien is gone. Whether he chose to block me from his side of the twin bond—which he rarely does—or something else has caught his attention, I no longer sense him enjoying this moment with Tandy and me.

I think I understand. Just as I used my tongue to mate our female as he wanted, a flash of another male—a human male, *Jared Turner*—crossed my minds' eyes before I banished it as quickly. Knowing Damien, he might not have been able to do the same. He feels the need to go after him, but Damien... he wouldn't do so. Not when it's so important to claim Tandy as our own so that we no longer have to worry about any male that came before us.

Still, I'm stunned he disappeared from our twin bond so suddenly which is why, when Tandy pats the nest and says, "Okay. I'm ready. Let's go," I'm too distracted to understand what she means by that.

After shaking it once, I tilt my head at her, my confusion clear.

She blows out a breath. "Really, Lucian? You act like you're a clueless virgin or something. Get on over here. I'm ready now."

A virgin… Ah. "You are correct, dear one. I have never mated with a female before."

Tandy goes still. "Hang on. Didn't you tell me you were, like, three thousand years old? Older than freaking Jesus? And you're still a virgin?"

Why does she seem so surprised? I understand that humans do things differently, courtesy of Haures, but in Sombra… "I was waiting for our mate."

We were waiting for our mate.

A wave of regret washes over me. As much as I want to experience further pleasure with her now—and she seems more than eager to finally receive our cocks—I really should retrieve my twin.

"If you are ready for your males, I need to get Damien and invite him to join us."

Tandy hesitates. She doesn't hide herself from me, though she does sit up. "Wait. You weren't kidding? You really want me to fuck you at the same time? You and your gloomy brother?"

I nod. "Yes. Only when you take us at the same time after you've accepted our essence will we be able to finalize our bond."

Her flat brow wrinkles. "That's right. That mate bond thing. Look, we can do that later, okay? Right now, I need to see if your real cock feels as amazing as what you did with your tongue. So if you're good with giving up your V-card with me, I'm so ready." She scoots back again, patting the nest in invitation. "Let's go."

"But Damien—" I begin. I must find him. She is *our* mate—

"He'll get a turn, Lucian. I promise. It's just sex. If he wants to fuck me later, I'll fuck him, too. You want to discuss some freaky twin threesome you guys are really set on? Fine. Just... I need you now. Like, *now* now."

She *needs* me. How can any male refuse their female when she needs them?

I step toward her. "I am your male. So is Damien. But he is not here and I am, and I will never leave our mate wanting if I can pleasure her."

Damien will understand. I cannot bond her to me without him, but just like mating her cunt with my tongue, I will now do the same with my cock if that's what she asks of me.

"Yes. Yes. Pleasure me. Fuck me. I don't care. But whatever you did to my pussy with your tongue, do it with your dick. Okay? 'Cause you did something, right? I could *feel* it."

Slowly, giving Damien time to realize what I am about to do without him, I stalk toward my waiting mate. I scent her need on the air, my mouth already watering for another taste, and if I exist for another three thousand years, I will always remember the way her pretty pink cunt glistens for her male on his first approach.

"I gave you my shadows," I tell her.

She props up on her elbows, her dim eyes fixated on my solid red cock. "What?"

I show her. In between one step and the next, I command my shadows to take shape, turning my demon cock into one that is made of pitch-black shadows that are slightly hazy and as sensitive as my tongue was when I plunged it inside of her.

Her eyes go wide. "And doing that to your tongue made me feel like I was having, like, three consecutive orgasms in a row?"

Is that why she screamed? From pleasure? Gods, I hope so... "Yes, dear one."

"Then get your ass over here with that shadow dick, Lucian, and give it to me."

Tandy waits for me. I pause at the edge of the nest, reaching out for Damien, letting him know that it is urgent.

There is still no answering tug on our twin bond. I frown, and I realize too late that I shouldn't have done so. Our mate mistakes my concern for my twin with a reluctance to mate her, and I sense her pain a split second before her legs start to close.

"Know what? It's okay. I shouldn't be so damn pushy. If you don't want to do this—"

I lay my hand on her knees. "I want to. Very much."

She shudders but leaves my palm against her much cooler skin. "You're so hot. And, okay, I definitely am attracted to you guys and your demon-y looks now, but your hand. I mean, you're *hot*."

"We are from Sombra," I coo, easing her legs apart so that I can crawl between them. "We are shadows, but we are also fire. We are heat. So are you, dear Tandy."

Reaching up, she runs her hand through her hair. "It's this mop, right? Fiery redhead, huh?"

Bending her legs so that I can fit my bulk in the cradle of her body, I shake my head. "Hair does not make one full of fire. Heart does. Essence does. Though," I say, gulping slightly as I fit my cock at her entrance for the first time, "I must admit... red is my favorite color."

Before either of us can decide that we should't be doing this, I push a little. My shadow cock glides easily inside of Tandy until our groins are flush, my body seated inside of her so completely, I never want to leave the sanctuary of her cunt again. She throws her head back against the nest, screaming again, and this time I'm sure it's because of how much pleasure I'm giving her.

Staying where I am though every nerve in my body begs me to move, I wait for her to open her eyes once more.

It takes a few moments before she does. Tandy

smiles up at me as she gets used to the sensation of my body filling hers, my hands bracketing her shoulders, my body shadowing hers. Then, in an instant, I change my mind. If I live another three thousand years, I will never forget the way her lips twitch in amusement mingled with pure affection as she raises her hand, placing it over my heart.

Her skin is pale, but compared to mine, it seems slightly pink as she stretches her fingers to stroke my nipple. "Red's my favorite color, too,"

Bending my head, I kiss her mouth because her cunt is stuffed full of my cock.

She giggles against my lips. "Thanks, Lucian. I was just dying to know what my own pussy tasted like tonight."

Withdrawing my cock because I can no longer bring myself to stay still, I thrust back into her tightness, enjoying her delightful little squeals as my shadows caress her cunt from the inside out. "You taste delicious, Tandy."

"I'm glad you think so. Your dick is pretty freaking awesome, too. You keep moving like that, I might have to stick around."

She's teasing. I can tell from both her tone and her essence. And yet, that doesn't stop me from reminding her, "You are our mate, dear Tandy. This is your cock. No one else will ever have it. It belongs to you."

"Yeah? Then go ahead and let me have it."

I've never been able to resist a dare. Not from Damien, and not from our mate. Following the movement of her hips, treating mating like a dance, I give her everything I have to offer—except for forever, but I cannot do that without my twin.

The entire time I'm mating our female, I choose to keep our twin bond open. I want Damien to be a part of this moment. Tandy is as much his mate as she is mine, regardless of my twin's secret beliefs, but even as I brace my arms after I finish giving her my seed and as much essence as I can spare to strengthen our growing bond, I notice something about the one I share with my brother.

He didn't cut me off or block me. It takes more essence than he'll let me share with him to do that as completely as he has. But he's missing all the same.

And though the last thing I want to do is wipe the lazy, sated expression off of our dear Tandy's face after I made her scream from pleasure again and again, I have no choice.

She must know the truth.

"Damien—"

"Mm. What about him? 'Cause I wasn't kidding. If he wants to come in, okay. I might need a second to recover from the fucking of a lifetime you just gave me, but I'm down."

I want nothing more than Damien to claim our mate the way that I just did.

But he can't.

"Damien... he's *gone.*"

CHAPTER 9
JARED TURNER

TANDY

Right after my demons grabbed me by the hands and brought me to Sombra, all I wanted to do was go back home.

Why? That's a good question. If I'm being honest with myself, it's not like I really had anything to go back *to*. My gig as the closing act for the nostalgia show only ran until the third week of January. After that, I didn't have anything lined up.

I'd sublet out my apartment in New Jersey when I got the stipend to stay in the hotel so I'd be close by to do drop-in appearances at the club's whim. Because I thought I'd book another job in the city, they have it through May, so I'm technically homeless at the moment since I sure as hell can't afford my hotel room without the stipend.

My 'friends' are all hangers-on or ex-lovers. My family is nonexistent. No matter how old I get, I can't shake the scandal that derailed my life.

I wanted to be just like Whiskey Rose. The platinum albums, the fans screaming my songs back at me, the movie deals and endorsements... I wanted that to be me. One big mistake later, and I'm a has-been and a punchline.

But in Sombra... it doesn't have to be like that. So there's no delivery. No shopping malls. No internet or phones.

There are also no judgmental stares. No whispers everywhere I go. No sense of failure dogging my heeled steps.

It took me a couple of days to come to that conclusion. Most of that was because, at first, I was just so fucking stunned that anyone would want me so badly, they'd whisk me away to another realm, then spend their every waking moment trying to tend to all my needs in a bid to convince me to accept them as my forever mates. What's especially amazing is that they're massive. Strong. Obviously *hung*. They're also demons, which gave me a pause at first, but besides the glowing eyes, ridges over their nose, and pointed horns, they're really not that different from human men. They believe I promised myself to them after I read that weird spell in the old book. If they chose to, they could do whatever they want to me, and it's not like I could stop them.

But they would *never*. I quickly learned that 'demon' doesn't mean 'bad' or 'evil'. They're just another kind of person, only one that is both full of magic *and* immortal.

And if I go along with it and let them mate me, I will be, too.

Lucian is *good*. Thanks to this essence exchange thing—which is basically them learning everything there is to know about Tandy Lewis with a simple touch—he knows just the right way to convince me to give him what he wants.

Immortality and a loyal demon husband? Not just one, either, but *two*?

Two true loves meant for me alone?

I made it, like, three days before I decided that, if you can't beat them, join them. I wasn't going back to New York. Not anytime soon, at least, and really? It wasn't that big of a loss.

But if these two wanted to take their turns with me? I'd be lying if I said I wasn't interested. Completely full of shit if I tried to pretend that I wasn't curious, or that something about their demon features didn't rev my engine a bit.

Add that to the dreams I have... dreams or maybe *visions*... every time I close my eyes and, hell, I'm only human. There's only so much I can resist. A demon who looks at me with his mismatched eyes as if he worships the ground I walk on? Who talks to me like a person, not a conquest, brings me food, offers me anything, and takes my hand as if I'm precious?

I knew I was going to have my way with Lucian sooner or later. Of course, because I'm Tandy Lewis, it ended up being sooner if only because I needed to lick my wounds a little after Damien's obvious rejection.

I kissed the other twin, and he walked away. I made the first move, and he told me to eat, then disappeared.

And now *he's* gone.

Lucian's trying his best to hide it, but he is visibly worried about his brother. Snapping his fingers, the two of us are dressed less than a minute after he realized Damien seemed to have vanished on us. Not in clothes, though; he's magic, but certain things like cotton and polyester are out of his wheelhouse. Besides, when you can use shadows to cover up, why not? It's quick, efficient, and it makes disrobing for sex super easy.

His eyes flash. Tongue darting out, he swipes it over his bottom lip, rumbling softly as though enjoying the last of my taste.

"I do," he rumbles, and just when I can't help but wonder again if he really can read my mind as well as see the future, he says, "It's your essence, dear one. Your scent becomes infinitely sweeter when you think of mating. And though there is nothing I want more than to return to your cunt again now that I've experienced the wonder of it, I must go."

I clutch his arm. Earlier, whenever I dared touch one of these demons, their skin was so feverish, I got the feeling I'd burn if I held onto them too long. Now? Something tells me that banging Lucian already changed me a bit because while he's warm, it's not so noticeable any more.

Or maybe that's just because I worked up a sweat myself as he fucked me...

I give him a squeeze. "Let me come with you."

He searches my face. "You are my mate, Tandy. *Our* mate. True, Damien hasn't mated you yet, but you are meant to be ours. You gave us your essence. You gave me your body. And still you want to return to your human world?"

Hang on—

"Is that where he is?"

"For our bond to disappear so completely, he had to have gone off-plane. We do not have the ability to open portals on our own. There wasn't enough time for him to find a mage to do it for him. That leaves only the human realm. We've been there before. Because of our bond with you, the pathway is open to us both. He must have gone to Earth."

And Lucian thinks that I want to hitchhike my way back there now.

Oh. Okay. I can totally see where he got the idea that I want to leave him then. Considering I spent my first few days nagging him to open that portal and ship my ass back to New York, it makes sense that my request to tag along with him would be seen as a sneaky attempt to go home.

Maybe before I had this moment with Lucian, I might've. Maybe if he didn't admit that Damien took off while we were obviously fucking. These two are the tightest pair of twins I've ever met; they're immortal demons who've been around for, like, three thousand years according to Lucian, so they *have* to be. If me getting it on with his brother was enough to send him not only out of their cabin, but out of their *world*?

Damn. Maybe I should've waited a couple of minutes for Lucian to grab his brother and start that threesome after all...

"This is my fault," I blurt out. "He left because of me."

"Yes. He did."

Wow. What happened to my sweet demon who calls me 'dear one' and caters to my every request? I really hope that wasn't just an act to get me to fuck him because, while it worked, it really sucks that he's not pulling any punches with me now that he has.

I release Lucian, stepping away from him.

The demon surges forward, cupping my cheek gently, leaving his claws as shadows while he caresses my skin. "No, Tandy. You misunderstand my bluntness. That was not my intent. To hurt you... I would never. But you are not wrong. Damien left, but not because you welcomed me into your cunt, dear one. If I mate you, it's almost the same as him mating you. But there is another..."

"Another?"

"Another male. One you've mated before. We've seen him."

Woof. One? I don't slutshame, not even myself, but the number's just a bit higher than that—and these demons *know*. It doesn't really bother me, especially since I just eagerly let him fuck me, too, adding to that number, but just in case, I ask, "The essence exchange thing tell you that?"

Lucian nods. "I can choose not to see things about your past that will only make me jealous and wish there was a way I could've found you earlier. I do that a lot. But Damien... he is a sensitive male."

Don't snort, Tandy. Don't you do it...

I choke instead. "Damien? Uh... you mean, like, your twin who walks around with a stick up his ass? That Damien?"

Sensitive?

Lucian frowns. "I assure you, there is nothing lodged inside of Damien's posterior."

I wave my hand. "It's a human expression," I tell him. Note to self: he might understand English because of my essence, but he doesn't quite get the nuances yet. I purposely make it clearer. "I'm just surprised you call him sensitive when he acts like he'd be happier if I never intruded on you two."

"And that is why you must allow us to give you our essence," Lucian tells me. "Because, my dear one, Damien wants you more than I do. And, I assure you, I want you very, very much."

Oh. I know that. I have the evidence of his 'want' currently making my inner thighs sticky.

But *Damien*?

"You sure?"

He nods. "I share essence with him. I know how he feels, even when he can't find the words to say it himself. Just like I'm beginning to understand that, in his own misguided way, he's decided the only way to convince you to stay with me is to get rid of any reason for you to return to the human world."

"He doesn't have to worry about that," I admit. "I'm pretty sure I don't have one."

"He believes otherwise." And then, to my shock, he says two words that change everything: "Jared Turner."

My stomach drops. "How do you know that name?"

"Because Damien thought it so loudly before he cut off our bond, it echoed into mine and rattled around my head before I shoved it aside to focus on your pretty pink cunt."

Bold. Holy shit, how did I never notice how bold

these demons are? Or maybe I did, but I liked how much Lucian showed me that he considers me his.

And Damien thinks the same thing?

He's jealous of *Jared*?

"We have to get Damien," I tell his twin. "I told you I'd give him a turn, right?" And I meant it, too. "Jared… he's a mistake from the past, that's all. You guys don't have to worry about him."

"I know that. And I should've went and retrieved Damien earlier before letting my own need for my mate send him away, but my dear Tandy… I think that's exactly what I have done."

I bite down on my bottom lip. "I don't get it."

Lucian shudders out a soft breath, then admits, "I think that Damien might have gone to confront him. This male who he believes owns your heart… and if this Jared has it, we never can."

Are you kidding me?

That's bullshit, first of all. Maybe demons don't quite get it since they only have this one true mate that they're searching for, but humans can love an infinite amount of people. I've given my heart away before to have it broken, smashed, stomped on, and I still hold it tight, ready to share it with someone else.

Could it be these demon twins? Maybe.

Do I still love Jared Turner? Not a chance.

But does that mean he needs to get involved in this? When I don't even really know what *this* is?

No fucking way.

"What's he going to do to Jared?" I ask, more concerned about Damien than my ex.

Lucian thins his lips, fangs overhanging the bottommost one before he grits out, "I don't know."

And that scares the ever-loving shit out of me because, if there's one thing I've gotten used to when it comes to Lucian, it's that he knows *everything*.

IN THE END, LUCIAN REALIZES HE HAS NO CHOICE BUT TO let me go after Damien with him.

That one hundred percent has everything to do with me. I, uh, kind of freak out about the quiet twin going after Jared—and when it hits him that I'm actually worried about *Damien*, not my asshole of an ex, he grabs my hand, tears open a portal, and pulls me through it with him.

Right before we left, he quickly explained that while his purple eye means that he is a magic user in his world, it usually takes a different skill set to do portal travel like that. However, after I read that *verus amor* spell, I somehow created a rift between my world and his that he can access on his own.

That means, if I go back to Earth, he can always come after me. Because of the way both Damien and Lucian have my essence, Damien could take a trip to the human world—and, using my memories and the way I 'imprinted' on Jared, he could find *him*.

Only one problem, and it's a biggie.

I knew there had to be a reason why my demons felt the need to take me directly to their realm. I'm right. Turns out, Sombra demons aren't allowed on Earth. There's this guy called Haures, the demon duke of Sombra, and he has a bunch of rules.

The first one? No one from my mortal world is to ever know that demons exist. There have been slip-ups over the years—which would explain why my fellow humans talk about demons, and how we have legends of our own about them—with all offenders earning a pair of enchanted golden chains clasped around their wrists, and a stint in a demon jail... and that's if the duke is feeling merciful.

Otherwise it's death by shadows.

Seriously. Lucian warned me against leaving the cabin and making a break for it in the shadowy woods that surround the twins' cabin because, if I did, I was risking the demonic creatures that haunt those woods coming after me.

And while I might look like lunch to some of them, others might see a female and take me—and, unlike Lucian and Damien, they won't wait until I consent to have their way with me.

He didn't have to tell me twice. Between the two demons providing me everything I wanted while waiting for me to agree to be their mate and some crazy demon who would rip me in half, I knew I was better off sticking around here. Damien might be closed-off and more than a little scowly, but I would never want him to be tossed to the woods like that.

Especially if he gets in trouble because he has the wrong idea that I'm still in love with Jared Turner.

I can only imagine what he saw in my memories to believe that. Just goes to show that the essence exchange isn't exactly foolproof, that it's up to the individual to interpret what they see and sense about me, because Damien is about to throw his whole future away in order to make sure his brother has one.

Lucian doesn't come out and say it, but maybe I'm getting better at reading him because I... I *know* that's what he's thinking. And though he doesn't regret what we just did, he'll move past it because he needs to rescue his twin.

And I refuse to be left behind if I can help.

Like me, Jared is constantly traveling. That's why, when the portal spits me out in an unfamiliar room with hotel standard art on the wall and the sterile scent of a rented space in the air, I don't jump to the conclusion that we ended up in some random spot.

Especially when I hear a very familiar voice shouting nonsense and gibberish, fear coloring his voice all the way from another room.

Jared.

CHAPTER 10
MY DEMONS

I follow the noise because it has to lead me to my ex.

Lucian is right at my side. He already informed me that, in the human realm, it's expected to appear in the faintest form of their shadows they have. Close to a mist, if you didn't know he was there, you'd be hard-pressed to see him.

Me? I'm shit out of luck. If I had accepted his essence, he could've wrapped me up in his shadows, hiding me, too. But he's a twin. That means Lucian can't give me that essence unless Damien does at the same time. So though I'm completely visible and I'm pretty sure Lucian would prefer I hang back before we know what's happening, I lead the charge, and he's smart enough not to try to stop me.

I mean, this is *Jared*. I'm not afraid of him.

But one look at my ex-lover crouched down slightly, his back up against a corner, arms thrown over his perfectly-styled hair as a dark shadow—as *Damien*—whips around him, clearly terrorizing the human male... he's definitely afraid of one of my mates.

Any hope that Damien was following the duke's law by staying out of sight is completely dashed. Sure, he's not in that solid, red-skinned demonic form they have, but with his mismatched eyes blazing out of his inky-black shadows, there's no doubt that he's here, and that Jared has already seen him.

Shit. Shit, shit, shit.

What now?

I don't know, but when Jared's head jerks up, I realize that I made a major boo-boo.

I kind of said that out loud, didn't I?

Whoops.

Using his back, he pushes up off of the wall so that he's standing. He's still covering his head, though he shifts his arms so that he can find me standing on the other side of the room.

"Tandy? *Tandy?* Is that you? For fuck's sake, do you see this? Help me!"

I swallow the nervous lump in my throat. Then, I

lie. "See what? There's nothing there. Are you okay? What's wrong with you?"

Whether it's because of the fact that I'm here or that Lucian is, or that he's been caught, Damien's dark shadows fade until, like his twin, he's barely visible. I still sense him, though, and he hovers close enough to Jared that he can swoop down on him again at a moment's notice.

I have to diffuse this situation. I have to find a way to explain what happened that won't get Damien in trouble, then get out before Jared realizes that me even being here is impossible.

"Was it a bird? You know better than to leave a window open in the city." Here's hoping he's actually still *in* the city—and that he's still thick and self-obsessed enough to buy my explanation. "All kinds of riffraff can get in."

He straightens. His gaze travels over me, from my 'just got fucked' hair to the slinky, black shadow dress that might pass as a LBD, only it's so tight, you can see *everything.* From the outline of my pussy to my nipples poking through the woven shadows—and my bare fucking feet—I can only imagine how I appear.

Like a former lover desperate enough for a taste that I'd show up unannounced at his place like I'm ready to seduce him so we can have sex.

If I invite him to the bedroom, he will follow me. I have no doubt about that. But since it seems like *I'm* the desperate one, he'll get his kicks knocking me down first before getting me on my back.

That's what Jared Turner does, after all.

He straightens up, running his finger through his hair as though trying to shake off the terrified state I found him in. A second later, and you'd never guess he was anything other than the sleazy pop star that he's spent the last fifteen years fronting as.

"Speaking of riffraff, Tan... I thought you learned your lesson. Breaking in to see me? Didn't that earn you your first probation?" He smirks, and I can't help but wonder how I ever thought of him as so handsome, I'd throw my friendship with Sierra away for his grin.

He's not wrong. I was wild in my youth, and more reckless than I should've been. I didn't take the break-up with Thr33peat *or* Jared well. With the band going away and my life falling apart, the rumors of Jared fucking Molly May on the side broke me.

So I broke into the hotel where they were in bed together, got really pissed, smashed some stuff, and got my ass arrested. His manager pressed charges so that Jared could keep up his image as a golden boybander, and the story told to the press was that I couldn't accept it when he broke up with me, so I attacked him and his new girlfriend.

It was the perfect PR move. After the fallout he endured for cheating on Sierra, he got the public back on his side by painting me as the seductress who tempted him away from his true love, and the insane ex who couldn't take it when he tried to find love with someone else.

I became the villain in both stories, Jared's rep got cleaned-up, and it only received another boost when, out of the kindness of his heart, he 'convinced' his manager to drop the charges.

But not until my mug shot was splashed all over the papers and blogs, of course.

Like, honestly? How did I ever think he was charming? How did I ever fall back into bed with him again and again, even while knowing I was his second choice whenever Sierra turned him down for the umpteenth time?

Because I was lonely. Because I was desperate.

Because he had a hold on me...

Not any more.

Jared chuckles, completely unaware what's really going on here. It's like he somehow forgot all about he was being cornered by Damien in his shadow form a couple of moments ago, but if that means my demon didn't break that stupid first law, I'm cool with whatever caused Jared to suddenly forget. I'll make my excuse to leave before he starts to get suspicious about what I'm doing in his hotel room uninvited, Lucian and Damien will come back to Sombra with me, and everything will be a-okay—

And then Jared just has to go on and say, "Tandy

Lewis. Damn. Look at you. Still think you're twenty, huh?"

It's the way his smirk reaches his tone. It irks me even more, and though my demon twins are still hiding in their mist forms in this room, I only have eyes for Jared as I glare over at him.

"I've grown up, Jared. I've moved on."

"Sure you have."

I fist my hands at my side. "Screw you. Know what? This was going to be *my* year. Sierra and I finally patched things up." Kinda. "I'm getting jobs, Jared." Before I found out I was meant to be a pair of demon twins' mate. "I'm doing better. Definitely better than *you*."

"You said that same shit when you were twenty-one," he says, laughing. My blood fucking *boils*. "Twenty-four. Twenty-seventy. The big three-oh. I guess, at thirty-two, maybe this could be your year. I wouldn't hold my breath, though."

"You're such a fucking *dick*—"

"Oh," he says, stalking toward me as if I hadn't just caught him cowering and whimpering, like, two minutes ago, "I know that. That's something you've always like about me. Being a dick." He drops his hand to his crotch, squeezing himself. "Sucking my dick. *Fucking* my dick. Huh, Tan?"

Off to the side, Damien *growls*. How do I know it's Damien? No clue, but I'm sure of it.

Uh-oh.

Jared frowns, glancing in that direction. "Okay. So maybe that was a bird flapping around the room before, but what the hell was *that*? You bring a dog with you when you decided to break into my place tonight?"

Shit. So he's still on me breaking in—which I did—and now he thinks I have a dog. And while that's better than Jared realizing there are two demons in the room with him... "A dog? What? No."

To my surprise—and relief—Jared shrugs. "Doesn't matter anyway. You're here. You're a month late to answer my texts, but since you went to the trouble to figure out what condo I rented now that I'm back in New York again, I forgive you. Let's fuck."

A *month*? Time must run differently in the demon world or something because, at my count, it hasn't even been a full week since New Year's Eve.

Whatever. That's something to deal with later. For now—

Before Damien can growl again, I shut Jared down. "I'm not here to sleep with you."

"Why not?"

Maybe because my legs were still quivering from the orgasm Lucian gave me as I walked into this room?

I don't tell him that. Instead, I say, "Because I'm too good for you."

It's true. It was always true. He used my own insecurities against me, then proceeded to wield them for the next twelve years. Whenever I was weak—at twenty-one, at twenty-four, at *thirty*—he was there, to fuck me and use me and discard me.

You know who won't do that?

My demons.

I scoff, then turn away from Jared. "I was always too good for you. It just took me to right this second to see it. But I see, Jared. I see a lot now."

And I have the doppelseers to thank for that.

Am I a psychic, too, now? Those dreams of mine... maybe they are visions. Or maybe it's wishful thinking that has me imagining Jared getting old and wrinkled, still making moves on women half his age, never finding true love... while I spend the rest of eternity with my demons.

I see it. A glimpse of the future, a flash of the happily ever after I always wanted... I see it, and suddenly all I want to do is go back to Sombra, curl up with Lucian, and get to know Damien better.

That's my fate. It might not have been the new year I planned, but my future will be better because I *see* it and I cling to that promise of forever with Damien and Lucian as I start to walk away from Jared.

But my ex? He doesn't have magic like my mates do. He can't see the future, not like I'm beginning to suspect that I can; and wouldn't *that* have been much handier when I was younger and would've known better than to keep my distance from Jared.

He also seems to have forgotten all about the shadows that were terrorizing him and the growl that unnerved him because if he hadn't? He might've thought better than to lunge for me, grabbing my arm in a bruisingly tight grip.

"Hey. Where do you think you're going?"

I shake my arm. "Let me go!"

"No. You're here. I'm horny. We're going to fuck. You know you want to. You know you want me."

I do *not*.

"Jared, get off!"

The air shifts. It's charged with something I can't quite explain, only that I'm suddenly far calmer than I was two seconds ago.

"Release the female," booms a familiar voice.

My head whips around. So does Jared's.

It's Damien. He's not even in his shadows. Fully manifested in his seven-foot-tall demonic form, horns arching, eyes blazing... he glowers down at Jared.

Jared lets go of me even as he says, "What the fu—"

"Now, Damien," orders Lucian from somewhere behind me.

Damien didn't even wait for the command. As Jared starts screaming, Damien grabs one of the chintzy awards from by the TV that Jared packs with him and carries wherever he goes as some sort of validation. Crossing the distance easily, he cracks it over the back of Jared's head, then backs away from Jared.

From *me*.

Jared crumples as Damien moves to the other side of the room. The screams stop, but I can't help but gasp.

"Holy shit, Damien! Did you *kill* him?"

"For speaking to you in such a manner, I should have. But, no. He will sleep, and when he wakes up, he'll have a bump on his head and the absolute certainty it was all a dream. But if he thinks to use his tongue against you in any way, his head will ache again, and he'll know better than to offend you."

I stare at him, stunned.

Firstly, that is the most Damien has said to me since we've met. Secondly? I'm sold. This demon came all the way here to warn my ex away from me, and when Jared ran his mouth, Damien didn't just take care of it with his brute strength.

Using their magic, he's going to accomplish what I never could: getting Jared Turner to leave me the fuck alone.

I dash around Jared's prone body, then fling myself at Damien.

He's in his shadows now that he doesn't need to threaten Jared any longer, but that doesn't stop me. I've learned that, go about an inch or two past the hazy outline of a shadow demon, you'll find flesh. I do now, throwing my arms around him, squeezing him tight.

For a split second, I think he's going to slither out of my grip. Maybe this much physical affection is too much for him. He freaked out a bit when I tried to kiss him, and this hug is definitely more intimate—but he doesn't.

And when Damien hesitantly lifts his arms, returning my hug, I let myself melt against his shadows.

Damn it. It feels right.

It feels like home.

They feel like home.

So when I finally pull away from him again—the first to break the embrace—I offer a hand to each of the demons before telling them, "Let's go home."

Because Sombra?

I think that's my home now, too.

CHAPTER 11
PROMISE

LUCIAN

I have never seen Damien so close to going fully demonic than I did when he was in his shadows, swooping over the human male, frightening him —until he manifested fully in front of Jared Turner after the *jamda* insulted our Tandy.

Even so, Damien was still my brother. Still *good*. He wouldn't hurt the male, not if he believed it would cause pain to our Tandy, but I knew what he was doing. Certain mages have the ability to remove memories from human minds. There is Sammael, Haures's former head mage, who was gifted in the skill. He could take memories, implant memories, do everything he could to keep the secret of Sombra and its demons hidden from the humans.

There was a hunter. Nox. I saw his future many times, though when we invited him to our cabin to offer him a prophecy, the stubborn hunter refused us. His mistake. I could've warned him that I saw chains in his future for visiting his human mate before she was mature enough to accept him, and that after his long imprisonment, he would find his way back to her—but when he did, he needed to be wary of the strange vessels that the humans use to get around since they can't do shadow travel.

There's a price to pay for those who ignore the doppelseers. Nox no longer has control over his forms, though he's been happily mated to the duchess's kin these last two decades so he doesn't mind paying it.

The same with Loki, a former student of the School of Mages. He stole the matefinder spell and cast it centuries before his human mate was destined to be born. The spell backfired, turning him fully demonic. And though we saw he would recover in time, it wasn't easy—and if he hadn't been too proud to accept the doppelseers' vision, it might have been.

For ages, we have kept an eye on those males whose futures were entwined with the prophecy that would either end existence in Sombra as we know it, or if we can change it, ensure prosperity and eternity for anyone who calls it their home.

It is Tandy's home now. Watching her run to

Damien, not knowing how close he was to losing the last of his essence and reverting completely to a mindless mass of shadows... watching our mate wrap her arms around him, searching for his embrace, before offering me her hand to guide her back to Sombra... this is her home.

We are her mates.

I want to finalize our bond as soon as we return to the cabin. The gold moon approaches, and my certainty that we need to be fully mated before it completes its ascent has grown stronger and stronger since Tandy summoned us to her.

She already accepted me once. Her essence tells me that she's ready to accept Damien now.

If she takes her twins together, we can give her our essence at last, then follow it with the mate's promise. There will be no severing our bond after that, and with it nearly irreversible, I should be able to see any future involving our mate once she is truly *our* mate.

That's all I want. If the shadows come... if the rain comes... if the child comes... I will either work to change the prophecy, or I will flee to another realm with my twin and our mate. There is Brille Rouge. Soleil. Even Earth, if I must. It won't be Sombra, and my powers will significantly weaken without the shadows that have surrounded us since birth, but it was never about the powers for me.

It was about using them to protect our mate. I will do that however I can.

And if I have to protect her from Damien, I will do that if I must.

I knew how close he was to losing control.

But Tandy? She doesn't understand. The instance we return to the cabin and Damien makes some mumbled excuse to leave her bedroom, I don't have a vision. I don't need to. The pain of rejection in her essence is too potent to ignore.

She hides it. With a laugh and a smile, she says he must have other plans and that's okay. She'd like a bath. Something to eat. A nap.

Privacy. Our mate needs privacy, and I will always give her what she requires.

So I do. I let Damien slip down the stairs to the main floor of our cabin without stopping him. Through our twin bond, I know he hasn't gone far, so I conjure the water at the temperature Tandy prefers. I wave my hand, the shadows falling away from her body. I only give her a fleeting, heated glance as I remember how I held her naked form against me not that long ago, then I swallow roughly.

"Rest, dear one," I say softly. "Take your bath. Sleep if you like. I will bring you something to eat."

Her smile is both sad yet wistful. "Whatever did I do to deserve a great guy like you, Lucian? You're so good to me."

Because you are my mate.

Because you are my life.

Because I love you...

My claws twitch as I realize that, for the first time since Tandy's been in our home, did I think of her as mine.

Not Damien's, too. Just *mine*.

But she isn't. She can't be. She belongs to both of us —and as soon as I make something worthy of her to eat that isn't simple bread and cheese, I will remind both Damien and myself of that fact.

I FIND DAMIEN OVER THE STOVE. IN ONE COOKING vessel, he's brewing a tea. At first, I think he realized how close he came to losing the last of his essence and started the ashbalm potion that bolsters our twin bond.

But then I sniff it, and say, "*Ergol.*"

"For Tandy. It'll help calm her. After the way that male spoke to her, I thought she might need it."

No. What she needs is the support of her true mates, but before I snap that at Damien, it hits me that this *is* his way of supporting her.

He will always tend to emotions first. I deal with the tangible. Things I can touch. I can do. I ran her a bath. I fluffed her bedding to make it more comfortable. I came downstairs to get her something to eat...

Damien has already done so. There is a hash made of *tybirs, ungez* meat, and herbs sizzling on the pan. It smells both delicious and comforting, and between that and the *ergol* tea, Tandy will feed both her belly and her heart.

I nod at my twin. "You should serve her. I think she would appreciate it."

Damien shakes the pan so that the meat doesn't stick. "I'd rather you did, brother."

"Damien—"

He glances at me. My claws cut into the flesh of my palm as I squeeze my fist.

His purple eye is *white.*

My twin is no longer my twin. If I looked in a scrying glass, would my eyes both be purple? I won't look. I *can't.* But if his eyes are white like those mindless creatures that can't escape the shadows, how is he standing there so calmly? He's speaking in the English language because we both know it makes Tandy feel more comfortable since she does not yet understand Sombran. A fully demonic male has no essence, but he is able to access Tandy's.

Our twin bond is barely there. I only hope the fledgling one that stretches between my twin and our mate is enough to keep him from losing the last of himself.

"Damien?"

"She will choose." His lyrical voice has gone flat. "I have sensed it."

No. I refuse to believe that. "We are the doppelseers. What I see, you see, brother. And what you sense, I know."

Damien steps away from the stovetop. "Look into your heart, Lucian. And ask it why it hides this vision from you. Your eyes might see, but your mate's essence blinds you."

"My mate? She is *our* mate."

What happened upstairs was a fluke. A fleeting moment made up of relief that Tandy is back in the cabin, and hope that she'll never want to leave again. She is my mate, but she isn't *mine*. She is *ours*.

If only my twin would agree.

His white eyes dim. "We are an abomination," he whispers. "Essence split between two males. Cursed to see... cursed to *know*... and I know that our Tandy is *your* Tandy. She will choose. And she will not choose the demonic twin."

"You are not demonic," I tell him.

"No?" His eyes flash. "I gave up the last of your essence when I opened the portal to the human world. I knew it was a risk. I knew that Haures would be able to tell I left. You weren't supposed to come after me."

I wasn't.

Moving toward him, Damien stays still as I lay my

hand on my twin's shoulder. "You are my twin. The other half of my essence. I will always come for you."

He shakes his head, then shakes off my hand. "Promise me. Promise me that, when the shadows claim me, you won't follow me there."

"Damien. Brother. I can't do that. Don't ask me—"

"You must, Lucian. For Tandy's sake, if not for the years that we've spent together as the doppelseers. I've never asked you for anything before now. So promise me. Promise me that you will keep her safe, and when I can no longer be trusted around her, you'll let me go and not follow."

"I—"

"Please," he says softly—and my heart breaks for the pain in his voice. "It will happen. Whether you see it or not, it *will* happen. I love you, brother. You've given me more than I ever deserved. I never asked, but I never had to. You were generous enough to share. With me. With Sombra. Just this once, be selfish."

I shake my head. "You ask for too much."

"I know. And you are the good twin, Lucian. You will give it to me just like you've given me everything else. So, please, *promise.*"

I can't use my gift to see a clear future that includes me, Damien, or Tandy. I never have. They've either been hazy or mere glimpses of images that flash too quickly to actually *see.* That doesn't stop me from trying now, but when all I see is black, I'm not sure if it's because the gods are hiding what will happen to the three of us from me entirely—or I am.

One thing for sure?

Damien is correct.

There isn't anything I won't give him.

So I shudder out a breath. "I promise."

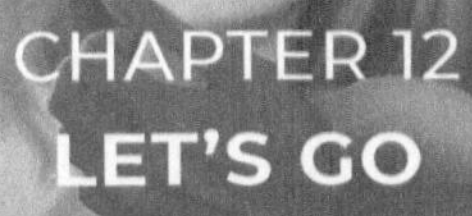

TANDY

As much as I want to grab Damien by the horn, pull him into my room—that, if everything goes according to plan, will be me and my demons' room before long—and show him just how hot it makes me to have someone stand up for me, I only just manage to resist the urge.

I haven't forgotten the way that Damien couldn't handle a kiss. It makes more sense now that I compare it to Lucian's reaction, and everything that happened at Jared's place. It's obvious that my demons have never been kissed before. If Lucian was a virgin, I'm betting Damien is, too. I have to remember that.

Plus, he seems to have this idea that he needs to

step aside so that me and Lucian can be together. Bull-shit. They promised me twin mates. I want twin mates.

I just need to wait until Damien comes around.

I won't push him. That's not fair to him, and no matter how hot and bothered I am, that doesn't mean I have to twist someone's arm to get them to sleep with me. Even though Lucian promises again and again that Damien, deep down, knows that the three of us are fated, he's struggling because he wants me so badly, but he doesn't seem to think he deserves his own happy ending.

It has everything to do with their weird eye thing. In Sombra, the colors mean something. Lucian taught me about them since, if I'm staying, it's good to know what kind of demon I'm facing when I eventually leave the cabin. The red-eyed demons are fierce hunters. The green are part of the demon duke's guard and soldier class. Purple obviously means they have magic powers. Gold is the common color, assigned to crafts-men, farmers, and those who don't fit the other categories.

And if I ever see blue eyes on a Sombra demon? I need to grab one of my mates because that's Duke Haures himself.

But white eyes... white eyes only belong to crea-tures that don't have essence. Kind of like animals in the human world, or evil pricks that don't have a soul. That's how I understand it. The prey beasts that we eat

—and I've never contemplated becoming a vegetarian more than when it hits me that I'm eating weirdo shadow critters—have white eyes. Demons that actually turn *demonic*... they have white eyes, too.

There are no other twins in Sombra. Lucian explains that to me. And it's not because they're super rare, either. It's because, when a demoness gives birth to identical twins at the same time, only one gets essence. The other is basically left in the shadows to perish.

That's what was meant to happen to Damien. Only Lucian—good from the start—recognized the twin bond from birth and split his essence. It was enough that they both have powers, they both can share a mate, and their mismatched eyes tell their story in a way I never understood until now.

No wonder he believes that I should be Lucian's mate, not both of theirs. After spending three *thousand* years knowing that you were marked for death, but only existing because of the generosity and love of your twin... when Lucian makes it clear that the one thing he's ever wanted was his mate, why wouldn't Damien believe that it would be the ultimate sacrifice on his behalf to try to pair me and Lucian up without him?

Lucian doesn't want that, though. As demon twins... as the doppelseers... he's always known that he would share his mate. I might've been iffy about the idea in the first place, but screw it: I'm on board now.

All we have to do is get Damien to realize that we can't be complete without him, and if I have to take one for the team and give him a little one-on-one attention first so he knows he's not simply a consolation prize, I think I can do that.

Unfortunately, patience has never been my strong suit. And when a couple of days pass when Lucian is the only twin who comes up to see me, I can't take it any more. Damien went after Jared for me. He cares about me, even if he can't show it.

If he can't, I *will*.

One thing I learned about the doppelseers that was obvious from the beginning is that Lucian is the face of their operation. Whenever he has a prophecy to share with one of the demons in this world, the crazy moving house we live in starts heading that way. At first, I thought I was nuts. I could've sworn I felt it drifting along, and Lucian finally admitted that the cabin can travel the length and breadth of Sombra on its own.

It's hidden, too, so as long as I don't leave it, I'm safe. But while I agree to do so until I'm more familiar with their world, Lucian refuses to invite anyone inside while I'm here. He deems it too risky, so when he visits villages to do his duty as the doppelseer, he leaves— and Damien stays behind with me.

I was waiting for an opportunity like this. Once

Lucian kisses me goodbye, then regretfully heads downstairs before leaving the cabin, I wait until I see him disappear into the shadows, then go down myself.

Sombra is made up of shadows. Of shadows and ash, fire and a heat that I'm still getting used to. Not all of the shadows are dangerous, though, full of the creatures that could hurt me. Only the edge of the shadows —the deepest, darkest parts of Sombra where their *two* moons can't even reach—are threatening to demons and humans alike.

So though my heart jumps every time Lucian slips into the shadows to visit a local village, I know he is safe. He will also return quickly, giving his prophecy, accepting gifts of gratitude, and hustling his way right back to me as though he can't dare to be separated from me and his twin for more than a little while.

I have one shot at this. If it doesn't work, I'll try again at the next opportunity, but my dreams... they've been changing lately. I still fantasize about my demons —especially now that I've had Lucian once, and instinctively know that that won't happen again until Damien's had a turn—but ever since me and Lucian had sex, I dream of one of my demons melting into the shadows, never to return again.

I don't understand it. I'm not sure I want to. But when I wake up, irrationally certain that those strange dreams will go away once the three of us are fully bonded... it makes me eager to take the next step with Damien before I lose them both.

The gold moon. It's grown larger, and though I know it's the night that anyone sleeping with their Sombra demon mate will end up instantly pregnant, I've watched Lucian track its recent growth as if expecting something else to happen that night.

Almost like it's our deadline. If I'm not their mate by then...

No. I've gone all-in. They want a human mate? Well, here's Tandy Lewis.

Let's go.

I FIND DAMIEN DOWNSTAIRS, HEAD BOWED OVER A STOVE that isn't lit.

His thick red fingers are clutching the edge of it, claws digging into the crystalline material that creates the demon cooktop. He doesn't turn to look at me, though his senses are so keen, he has to know I'm here.

Is he waiting for me to approach him? I can do that.

I tiptoe behind him, then when I'm right there, I run my fingertips down his solid back.

"Damien—"

His head whips around. Suddenly, he's baring his fangs at me, snarling, his white eyes blazing out of a face I don't know.

Because this... this is not Damien.

He's a *demon*.

No. Not a demon. Lucian is a demon. Damien is *demonic*, and as my shaky fingers fly to my face, covering my cry of surprise and anguish, I can't help but think I'm too late.

I lost him. Damien wasn't ever mine, not really, and I lost him.

Or did I?

His eyes are pure white, his features terrifying as he roars, but he strangles the sound as he falls back on his heels. Remorse washes over his face, and his roar becomes a howl of pain as he dissolves into his shadow form right in front of me.

I've noticed the holes strategically placed around the cabin before. Lucian told me they were ports for shadow travel. In Sombra, they can't quite travel through walls, but in their shadow forms, they can condense into a fine mist and freaking *fly* if they have to.

And that's exactly what Damien does.

I immediately run outside after him. It should be impossible to pick Damien's shadows out of the millions of others that make up this place, but ever since I was brought to Sombra, Lucian told me that the second spell I read in Sierra's apartment was a mating promise.

I gave myself to them, just like I did my essence

when they took my hands, and a bond was formed that could only be broken if I forsake them entirely. There would be no going back. No second chance. I'd never see them again, and since I didn't know what that meant for them having my freaking soul, I never went that far.

Then I started to like the idea of being their mate, and I decided I never would.

Did I believe there was a bond? Not really. Between Damien and Lucian, definitely, but between the three of us? Honestly? I figured that was just something he was saying to get me into bed at first.

Tell that to the way I feel something deep in my chest, pulling me in the exact direction Damien flew off in. Not only that, but I... I'm pretty sure I can see him.

I can go after him. I can explain, or I can apologize... something. But I can't just let him disappear into the shadows. He won't come back. I don't know why, but I'm sure of it. Losing Damien will break Lucian, too.

I can't let that happen.

CHAPTER 13
IN THE SHADOWS

TANDY

hree steps. I make it three steps past the threshold of the cabin before Lucian materializes out of the shadows, grabbing me gently and pulling me against his solid chest.

I immediately struggle, even though I know who has me. But I have to.

"Let me go, Lucian. Now!"

He does. As though he's also remembering the way that Jared grabbed me, setting Damien off, he immediately releases me once I tell him to.

I whirl around, pointing my finger up at his face. "What are you thinking, grabbing me like that? Damien just *flew* into the shadows. The *woods*, Lucian." The woods he warned me about, the ones right on the edge of the shadows. Because of freaking *course*. "We have to go after him."

Lucian's tone is mournful. "I cannot."

What? "Yes, you can!"

He shakes his head. "I promised him that, if this happened, I wouldn't follow him into the shadows."

And? "*You* did. I sure as hell didn't."

"Tandy—"

"Do you trust me?" I ask Lucian.

"Of course I do."

"Do you love me?" I demand.

"With everything I am," he vows.

I pat his chest. "Good. What about Damien? Don't you want him back with us?"

Lucian's chest is heaving under my palms. It's taking him everything he has not to toss me inside—or to go after Damien himself. "He is my twin. You are our mate. The gods decreed that we three were fated to be together."

I hold up my hands as I take a step away from him. "Hey. Can't go against the gods, right?"

"Tandy, please. Just wait a moment—"

I can't. "He won't hurt me." I believe that. Lucian... I can tell he wants to let me go save his brother—and there's only one way he will. "See the future, Lucian."

"I see red," he whispers. "Always red with you, dear one."

Red like my hair.

Red like human blood.

Okay, maybe not.

Too bad.

I shake my head. "Know what? I don't give a shit what you promised Damien. I don't give a shit what you saw, either. I'm Tandy. I'll always do what I think is right at the time. Sometimes that ends up with me in the backseat of a cop car, but oh well." I wave my hand. "I'm good now. And I'm getting Damien back. Will you stop me?"

Lucian's glowing eyes blaze into the shadows. "I will give you until the black moon rises," he grates out. "Then I'm coming for you, Tandy."

Fair enough. He promised his twin he wouldn't chase him. But he won't be going after Damien. He'll follow after me.

I blow him a kiss. "I'll be right back."

And I'm bringing Damien home with me.

I KNOW HE'S HERE. I *KNOW* IT. IT'S HARDER TO PICK HIM out of the shadows surrounding me since, everywhere I look, I see blinding white eyes staring back at me, but I *feel* him. In my chest, in my *heart,* I know that Damien is here.

I don't want to believe he's watching me without letting me know where exactly he is. That would be cruel, especially when any of the monsters in the shadows could attack me.

If he lets them eat me, I guess I'll know where we stand once and for all, huh? And maybe that's my panic talking, the overwhelming anxiety that the demon I've known for little more than a week could disappear out of my life as quickly as he entered it and *shatter* it.

And I do mean shatter. When Jared broke my heart, I pieced it back together. Same with every other love I've had before or since. I moved on. I showed the world that, no matter what, they'll never break Tandy Lewis. Even when it was my fault, and then when it wasn't, I always come back swinging.

But if we lose Damien... is there coming back from that? I thought the guilt I suffered for betraying Sierra was bad. It took me twelve years to get to the point where she actually attempted to reach out and mend our old friendship. But if I came between a pair of bonded demon twins who've been codependent for *three thousand years*?

No. There's no coming back from that.

So I just have to make sure that I do what I said I would and bring Damien home with me.

If he cares... if he really cares... there's only one way I can think to reach him. If he ignores me, I won't give up, but if he answers?

Then I'll know my protective demon mate is still in there somewhere.

Cupping my mouth, I call out, "Damien? I *need* you."

No response. I spin around, trying to find him in the darkness, and open my mouth.

Before I can shout again, the air shifts. There is no such thing as wind in Sombra; at least, not in the part of the shadows where we hide. So when my hair flutters around my face, my shadow dress wafting in the unnatural breeze, I'm hoping that the mass of shadows that just whipped around me is Damien and not one of the completely soulless demons who live out here.

Through the shadows, firm flesh finds me. Possessive hands land on my upper arms, shadow claws tickling me even as I feel the heat from the demon at my back. He's careful, though, very careful when he lifts me a couple of inches off the ash before turning me to face him.

It's dark as fuck in here. The only light comes from the white eyes gazing down at me, but it's enough. I'd recognize his inky black features and infamous scowl anywhere.

"You shouldn't have come," Damien says, voice as soft and lyrical as ever. "I don't want to hurt you."

This from the demon who handled me as easily as if I was a grown human maneuvering a toddler around? Please. Demonic or halfway there, I don't think he *can* hurt me.

"You won't," I say, lacing my voice with absolute certainty. "But, Damien... you're the one who's hurting. You don't have to. I can make you feel good." And then, because I *am* absolutely certain that this demon will never do anything more except reject me and hurt my feelings, I drop my hand, searching his shadows for the cock that has to be in there.

I find that, too.

It's hard. Heavy. As deliciously thick as his twin's which tells me that they really *are* identical.

It's also undeniably an erection which means that, even if he believes he's on the cusp of losing himself forever to the shadows, he is at least attracted to me.

Does he recognize me as his fated mate?

I squeeze. "I promise. I want this. I want *you*."

"You are Lucian's," he rumbles.

With my other hand, I cup his throat because it's about as high as I can reach while still holding onto his dick. My fingers dip an inch or so past his shadows, but the way his face tightens, his eyes closing briefly as though it feels as fantastic to him as it does me... I don't think he minds.

Especially when I add in a soft whisper, "I'm yours. I always have been, even if I was too slow to realize it. But until you claim me as your mate, you won't believe it. Will you, Damien?"

"If I do this, you won't be able to change your mind. If you choose Lucian—"

Is that what this is about? That he honestly believes that I would pick one twin over the other? Sure, Lucian is kind and sweet and I can talk to him for hours. But Damien? If I get to know him better—if he *lets* me—I'm sure I'll find things I can talk about with him, too. I already know his possessive side is perfect for me, and even if I had my doubts, Lucian loves him.

Lucian loves him, so why wouldn't I?

"I did choose Lucian," I remind Damien. But before he can walk away from me like I saw in my terrible dreams, I hurriedly add, "And this is me choosing you. It's the three of us, okay? Forever and ever, that's what I promised you. That's what I'm hoping you're going to promise me. But first... I need you, Damien. Don't you need me?"

Damien doesn't say anything right away. Then he moves so quickly that, for a hot second there, I think I fucked up. Like, *really* fucked up. That I misjudged him, and that he really did go demonic. The white eyes are throwing me—I didn't realize how much I got used to the purple one until now—and as he hoists me up, urging me to wrap my legs somewhat around his tree trunk of a thick waist, I think that fucking Damien might be the last thing I do.

And if it is? What a way to go...

But, no. I shove that idea out of my head before

Damien can pick up on it from my essence because he's not trying to get away from me. As he shoves my shadow dress up so that I'm naked from the waist down, it's the exact opposite.

He's not trying to get away from me. He's trying to get *inside* of me.

Can he see in the dark? I'm not sure, but it takes him a few moments before he's lodged the tip of his shadowy cock inside of me. Sensing the slight resistance because a) he's seven feet tall and he's *huge*, and b) I'm nice and wet, but he's attempting to fuck me standing up so that angle is different than in missionary, Damien hesitates.

Ah, *hell no.*

I shift my hips until I can take him myself. It helps that, as a shadow demon, Damien can control the shape and size of his shadows. When I've seen him or Lucian like this, it's like a hazy silhouette of their true features. But then I saw Lucian turn only parts of himself to shadow when we fucked, like his claws and cock, so I know they can control them.

Damien does now. Making his cock the perfect size to stretch me out completely without hurting me at all, he bottoms out inside of me as I cling to his biceps with my nails.

He roars again, only this time? It's a sound of pure pleasure that echoes in the eerily quiet shadowy woods. At the sound of him claiming me, the other white eyes wink out, leaving us completely alone.

Fine with me. I'm more than a little preoccupied as Damien—*my* Damien—begins to thrust.

As the roar dies out, the only sounds I hear are his soft grunts, my muffled moans as I bury my face against his chest, and the squeak as his shadow dick moves in and out of my soaked pussy. I can tell what he's doing. This isn't about pleasure, or about making love. Not really. That will come later, when it's me, Damien, and Lucian together, but for now?

He's doing exactly what I basically begged of him. He's claiming me as his.

So me? I just kind of hang on for the ride as he fucks me. But just like when Lucian was about to come the only time we had sex, the same strange thing happens as Damien picks up his rhythm: I start to come around his cock without anything other than penetration to get me to do it. And that's definitely more unexpected this time. Bless Damien's heart, but he's awkward, kind of stilted, and his movements are frantic as though he's hurrying to finish. I did expect this first round with the broody twin would be as quick as it was when I enjoyed Lucian's solid body, so I'm not all that disappointed when that same warmth floods my pussy as he climaxes inside of me, but that's only because I'm climaxing with him.

They'll learn. With Tandy Lewis as their mate, I'll

teach them about stamina in no time. About what I like, and how to make me come before they nut in me. Granted, for absolute beginners, Lucian managed to before—both when he fucked me and when he ate my pussy out—and as I squeal against his pec, Damien is doing it now, but just in case it's only beginner's luck, we'll have to work on it.

Hey. We have all eternity to get it perfect.

DAMIEN

For nearly three millennia, I clung to the essence that Lucian fed me through our bond so that I didn't disappoint my brother. But as I found completion inside of my perfect mate—*our* perfect mate—it isn't only my side that I share with her.

Releasing a breath as I fold her up in my arms, my cock still buried deep inside of her, I let go of Lucian's essence while transferring mine to Tandy.

It's purely instinctive. All demon males want nothing more than to perform the essence exchange. Taking that which your female offers you, giving her everything you are, everything you were, everything you will ever be... it's what we are made to do, and why the essence exchange is essential to finalize a demon mate bond.

I still must give her the mate's promise while pinning her between my twin and me. Though I whispered it to Tandy while I mated her just now, it won't actually complete our three-way bond until Lucian is with us.

He's already blessed her with his essence. I'd suspected as much when the essence I held onto all these years seemed to weaken without warning. I'd spent some, traveling to the human world to confront Tandy's former mate, but we are the doppelseers. We are powerful. We are bonded. If I used the essence and Lucian insisted on my return to Sombra, he would've passed me more.

But he couldn't. Not if he already gave everything he had left to Tandy during their mating.

I was content to slip away into the shadows and into madness. Once the tiny spark of essence I had left disappeared, so would I. But then my feisty human mate gave me a reason to continue my existence, and perhaps it makes me as selfish as I've long believed I am, but now she has essence given to her from both of her males.

I knew the moment she received it. Tandy gasped, both her eyes and her mouth going wide, and for a moment, they lit up before her lids shuttered close briefly. At the same time, she squeezed my length as her cunt pulsed around me.

As much as I didn't want to withdraw from her snug body, the way she squeezed me left me unable to do anything but explode. At least, that's what it felt like. I've rubbed my cock until it released seed countless times over the years, but now that it was being given to our mate at last?

I was unprepared for how amazing it felt, and as I lift her off of my spent cock, lowering her to her feet, I can't wait until I can claim her again.

But when I do? It will be with Lucian.

Tandy holds up her hand. "Give me a second. My legs are a little weak. Once I get the feeling in them back, we can go. Lucian's waiting for us. I'm pretty sure he can tell you're okay, that I finally got to mate you, and I'd put coin down that he'll be ready for another round almost immediately." She leans against me. "Is this alright?"

It's *perfect*.

My heart swells almost as much as my cock is prepared to do. Our dear Tandy... she's using my essence instinctively, isn't she? I didn't say out loud that I wanted to return to Lucian so that we can give her the mate's promise or that Lucian is prepared for our return, but she *knew*. Just like, courtesy of my essence, she now can speak Sombran...

I allow our mate to lean against me as long as she likes. Through our new bond, I also give her some of my strength. I'd offer to carry her if I didn't think her pride would have her refusing me, and when she says she's ready to go back to the cabin after mere moments, I nod and follow close behind her as she sets off.

This section of the shadows had emptied once I made my claim on my former mortal known. The smaller prey beasts might've been curious, but they know better than to go up against a male demon. As for any of the lost, fully demonic creatures that lurk in its depths... I have our female to protect. They would never best me to get to our Tandy.

Tandy leads the way. After a few steps, though, she pauses and I can sense her sudden curiosity.

"Hang on. How do I know the way out of the woods?"

I stroke my hand down as much of her back as I can reach. "Because I do, dear one."

She turns, raising the tiny strips of hair over her eyes. "Oh? You mate me and now I'm your 'dear one', too?"

Precisely. I'm so glad she understands. "You drip my seed, Tandy. That tells all of Sombra that you are now my mate as well. *Our* mate. You are both Lucian's and mine, and you are dear to us both."

Tandy shrugs. "Okay. Never thought I'd be 'One' again, but I like it." She nuzzles against my shadows, sending a renewed jolt of pleasure through me. In all my years, I never knew my shadows were as sensitive as they are, but though I can't wait to take our mate in my demon form, I will definitely remember that. "Even if you kind of lose sweet confection additions when you remind me I'm leaking arrival."

Now that Tandy has both of our essence, she's effortlessly speaking in Sombran, though I'm not so sure she's figured that out yet; that, or how she can navigate the woods because my memories are aiding her in doing so. I have, however, and it amuses me how her thoughts in English translate to my language.

She said something about 'brow-knee points' and leaking 'come', though I don't quite understand what she means by that.

So I ask. "Arrival?"

Tandy makes the most adorable face. "Arrival? What? No. I said 'arrival'. You know." She changes the pronunciation just enough that, now, it sounds harsher, like, "'Kum'?" She gestures under her dress. "Seed?"

Ah, yes. She knows I have marked her well.

I smile down at her.

Her face melts into one of pure delight. "I don't think I've ever seen you smile before," she says softly. "Looks good on you."

I drop a kiss to the top of her pretty red hair. I've wanted to put my mouth on her again since the day I panicked and fled from her quarters after she put hers on mine. This isn't her mouth since it's her hair, but our mate is right in her certainty that we will now have forever.

I'm not worried about the prophecy. Before, I was, but only because Lucian was afraid of something happening to our Tandy before we could finalize our bond. That was my being selfish again. So sure she would choose Lucian, I was prepared to wait for them to accept each other. Now I see that I should've given Tandy my essence and my cock as soon as she would've welcomed it.

Still, there is time. We are the doppelseers. With our mate to protect and her essence to bolster us, there isn't anything we won't be able to accomplish.

TANDY SEEMS SURE THAT LUCIAN IS WAITING FOR US IN the threshold of our cabin. She told me on the trek home that my brother only lingered behind because of his promise to me, and that Tandy used her human wiles to convince Lucian to let her run into the shadowy woods unprotected, but I will also remember to discuss that with my brother later.

What if I had been fully demonic? What if I could still turn? I know he has faith in me, but to risk Tandy? We can never allow any harm to befall our mate.

But she is right. Lucian is pacing along the threshold, but as though he used our bond to find us, he breaks for the shadows right before we exit them.

Tandy waves. "Look who I found."

Lucian comes to a stop. For a moment, I'm worried that he scents me all over our mate and has sudden regrets about sharing her. He never has, he's never given me any sign that he wanted Tandy as his own, but I am worried—

I shouldn't be.

He lets out a soft roar of his own, dashing over to us. After giving Tandy a quick, welcoming squeeze, he claps his hand on my shoulder.

"Brother. I can't believe it. Your *eyes*."

Tandy looks up at me. "Oh, shit," she says, slipping into English again in her surprise. "I didn't notice. Damien, your eyes are purple. Both of them." She swivels back so that she's facing Lucian. I already know what she's going to say before she blurts out, "You, too, Lucian."

Purple eyes. We both have purple eyes. As though we were born brothers instead of twins, we each have a matching set of mage eyes...

I would trade them. If it meant I had to carry the mark of the white gaze with me to keep Lucian as my twin and Tandy as our mate, I would trade them... and I know that my twin agrees.

Luckily, we don't have to. Luckily, Tandy *is* our mate... or she will be as soon as we claim her.

We no longer share essence. Not while it swirls around inside of our Tandy, but as my brother squeezes my shoulder wordlessly, I know exactly what he is about to do. How many times have we discussed this very night? Without being able to see what mating our female would be like, we imagined it, and now it's about to become a reality.

So when Lucian starts to lower his body to the ash, I follow him. As one, we go down on bended knee.

Lucian clears his throat. "Will you accept us as your mates?"

"Can we give you our mate's promise and make you ours?" I add.

Beneath the nearly full moon over our heads, Tandy's eyes might be a dull green shade, but they seem to sparkle as she holds out a hand to each of us. "Hey. I'm already pretty stretched out, and as lubricated as I can get. What better time to try taking two demon dicks at the same time?"

Tandy is small. She does not have the physical strength to heft us to our feet, but neither my twin nor I release our mate as we return to a standing position.

Neither of us starts for the entrance to the cabin, either, and she gives us another curious look.

"Oh, you thought I was joking? No. I'm not joking. I've been dreaming about this since I gave in and decided that you, you, and me... we're together. The things I've seen us do in my dreams... yeah, no. Let's go."

Only we don't. Not yet.

As my twin and I lock our purple gazes together, I know we're both thinking the same thing.

Is Tandy dreaming? Or seeing a vision?

Is our human mate a visionary like we are? By bonding the three of us together, will we be the trebleseers?

What will this mean for the prophecy no—

"Hey." Tandy snaps her fingers. "Chop, chop, fellas. Lucian? Do the hand-wavey thing and let's get the shadow clothing gone, yeah? Damien? Head upstairs and start fluffing that bean bag thing. If I'm being stuffed by my mates for the first time, we're gonna be comfy because once you guys get the first fuck out of the way to claim me, we're going to explore each other the rest of the night." Her lips quirk upward. "I'm a *very* vivid dreamer, and there are quite a lot of things I'm dying to try out."

***

EVERY SOMBRA DEMON KNOWS THE MATE'S PROMISE.

The demon duke of Sombra is the only known bondmaster existing in our realm. We asked him how our being twins would affect our mate bond and the promise. Haures believes that, if we say it exactly as it's been written since the beginning of time, we will bond our mate to us all the same.

But that's not what Lucian and I have ever wanted to do...

For as long as I can recall, we had an image of bonding our mate to us. Like Tandy's, it might've been something we fantasized over so often that now it's become our truth. It does not matter.

With Tandy between her two males, we finally have her where she belongs.

Lucian is sprawled out on his back, leaning into the well of the large nest that will always support the three of us while we mate and we sleep. Once we were all naked, our Tandy instructed him to lie down and turn to shadow. I watched in fascination as she climbed on top of him, their chests pressed together, as she slowly worked his cock inside of her cunt.

She writhed on top of him a few times, making sure he was completely seated before she arched her back, presenting her bottom to me.

Reaching behind her, Tandy uses her wee human fingers to spread herself open wide.

Our mate is stunning, but seeing her pretty pink cunt stretched around my brother's shadowy cock? I nearly spill, and I haven't even worked myself inside of her yet.

No. My seed belongs to Tandy, and before I lose control again, I lay my hand on her skin.

Before I took her earlier tonight, I noticed a chill whenever I dared a fleeting touch. Now? She feels the same as me, and when I start pushing the head of my cock inside of her, she's actually pleasurably warm inside.

I groan, and she echoes the sound. "That's it, big guy. Take your time. It'll seem tight, and the two of you might have to... um... adjust a little, but I can take you. I'm sure I can."

A flash of Tandy in a position similar to this, only with a pink cock in her cunt and one in her bottom flashes through my mind. I banish it just as quickly, swallowing my rising envy even as I slowly feed another inch inside of her newfound heat.

"You have done this before," I can't help but grit out.

She wiggles back, helping me by taking even more of my shadows. "Don't be jealous, Damien. I can promise you, while I've done a lot, taking two cocks at the same time in the same hole... this is a first for me. Throw in the fact you two are my demon mates and, oh yeah. Never done this before but, fuck me, we're going to do this all the time so long as you guys can make it so you fit just like this. The pressure and the *shadows...* fuck. I'm gonna come just like this."

I glance down as she continues away in English,

wiggling enough to create some sort of movement between our three bodies. To my amazement, she'd done just what she said she would: she's taken both Lucian and me at the same time.

It is impossible to thrust; at least, not the way I did when I was the only cock in her snug cunt. Tandy is doing all the work, pinned on our lengths as she is, but between the connection I have with our mate *and* my brother... I agree with Tandy. I am about to 'arrive' quite quickly.

Through our twin bond—because it seems as if my dear brother has been struck speechless by the sensations traveling through us—I can tell that Lucian agrees.

"Our soul will be yours," I promise Tandy in Sombran, beginning the modified mate's promise.

"Our heart is in your hands," continues Lucian, gasping out the words.

Taking pity on my brother for he didn't yet get to 'arrive' tonight, I say the next line of the vow: "Our lives will be forever intertwined."

At the same time, my twin and I finish the vow by telling our mate, "I give myself to you. We give you everything."

And as the bond between Tandy, Lucian, and I finalizes just as we both purposely release our seed inside of our mate in unison, that's exactly what we do.

CHAPTER 15
BILLIE IN NUIT

TANDY

Talk about a complete one-eighty.

As another lonely Christmas slipped by, followed only by the promise of what the new year could bring, I'd convinced myself that the most Tandy Lewis could ever hope for were booty calls and one-night stands that meant nothing more than just scratching an itch.

Commitment wasn't for me. At least, that's what I thought.

I was wrong.

Look at me now. I didn't just accept *one* fated mate for all of eternity. Oh, no. I have *two*.

And I don't think I could have chosen any better myself.

If you ask my demons, they'll insist that it wasn't my choice. Not really. Their gods blessed them with me, and while I could choose to bond myself to them or not, as soon as I read that true love spell and made the mating vow, I was theirs.

All I wanted was someone to love me. I got *two*, and they wanted me so badly, they waited almost *three thousand years* to fuck me for the first time. I didn't even know they were virgins when we met; I wouldn't have believed it if it wasn't for the fact that they'll never lie to me. Lucian was so eager to sleep with me when I initially propositioned him, and when I followed Damien into the woods, there was no hesitation. That demon pushed up my dress and guided my legs around his hips like he'd done it a million times.

Nope. It was just pure instinct and three freaking millennia of wet dreams that made them my perfect lovers.

They are perfect, too. They basically worship me. I have everything I want, plus the bonus of immortality because I agreed to let them bond themselves to me. As if I could refuse. No saggy tits ever. No grey hairs. I'll never grow old, they'll never cheat on me—or me on them—and I had the added bonus of watching Damien terrorize the hell out of Jared, then later conk my ex on the head before I finally could shove him out of mine.

Sure, the essence exchange itself isn't perfect. I had

to figure out a way to throw up a block inside my mind as soon as their existence filled it. Two demons times three thousand years, give or take? That many memories would break my brain, and I'm happy to move forward with my demons based on what I know about them so far.

And what I *do* know?

Is that they love me. They'll never stray. They'll be devoted lovers who will pleasure me until I'm boneless, then carry me to the tub where Damien washes my feet and Lucian lathers my back. There isn't anything they won't do to make me certain in my choice to accept them, and if I get a flash of two very familiar faces in my mind whenever their essence ekes out a little, I finally learn the truth about how far they went to get me to be their *forever*.

The gods gave me to them, but they had a little help. Turns out that my former bandmates—both Billie *and* Sierra, can you believe it—were tied by fate to a demon of their own. As powerful seers, Lucian and Damien could sense my relationship to my old friends whenever they ran into Billie or Sierra. Put them together, and for the first time, my demons could finally sense I was theirs, and that those two were the clue to my identity.

And my old friends?

They set me up. Sierra made contact with me for the first time in years so I would feel confident approaching her when the news about her pregnancy broke. Billie helped from the Sombra side since—surprise—she lives here with her mate. Between the two of them, they told my demons everything about me that they knew, and I wondered why they could guess exactly what buttons of mine to press to get me to react the way they wanted?

My essence helped, obviously, but so did my former friends.

For the next few days, I enjoy my new mates. Sometimes I focus on giving Damien my undivided attention, then Lucian, but most of all, it's the three of us together. Considering how I'm the focus of *their* attention when we are, I have to say, I much prefer it.

But I knew I'd have to face my friends eventually. And when it's *Damien* who suggests we take a trip to Nuit—the village where Billie lives and Sierra often visits—how can I refuse?

I can't, and away our moving house goes.

***

I'LL ADMIT IT: WHEN DAMIEN AND LUCIAN EVENTUALLY park the house on the edge of Nuit, marching into the village as they flank me on both sides, I'm more relieved than I should be that Sierra isn't currently in Sombra.

Though she's taken a back seat to superstardom,

Sierra still spends most of her time in the human world. Guessing how I would react when her pregnancy leaked—and she really is pregnant, just with a half-demon baby—she knew I would run right to her apartment. Just like how she'd known that I'd be nosy enough to grab the book and read the spell if she left a bookmark on the page, the grimoire left out on her coffee table.

Insane, isn't it? Lucian confirmed that, as his mate, I was a complete mystery to my demons until they took my hands and I inadvertently sent my essence over to him and his twin. But Sierra, a friend I'd been on the outs with for more than a decade, inferred from my teenage personality how I'd react as someone in their early thirties.

And, damn it, she was *right*.

I did everything she expected me to, and it was all on purpose. Both of my former bandmates were instrumental in helping me find my demon mates. I'm not so sure how I feel about that yet. Grateful, certainly, since I can't imagine spending the rest of my immortal life with anyone else, but would a heads-up have killed them?

Part of me wonders if keeping quiet about Sombra demons and my fated tie to Damien and Lucian was Sierra's way of getting back at me just a little bit. Now that I know she also has bonded to one of these magnificent males, that makes her just as immortal.

We'll have an eternity to hash out our past, and for me to make up for betraying her the way I did.

Call me a procrastinator, but I'm okay with waiting until maybe my third or fourth decade before begging my old friend for forgiveness again. I've tried, never blaming her for refusing to accept I was sorry, and I want to believe that it wasn't all just a trick to get me here that had Sierra reaching out in the first place... but while I'm in the honeymoon stages of bliss with my demons, I'd rather not bring up the past.

Though that doesn't mean no one else will...

Sierra isn't here, but Billie is. Standing next to a towering red-skinned male with *two* pairs of horns and glowering green eyes, she starts shaking her head the second she sees me.

Not in anger or pissiness, though. More like shock mingled with amusement that she's here, and so am I.

Living in this shadow realm looks good on Billie. Her skin is glowing, her big, bouncy, golden blonde curls surprisingly well-styled considering there's no product here unless Sierra is supplying her with some, and she's wearing a beautiful, handwoven dress that shows off her healthy figure.

To my surprise, she actually reaches out and grabs my arm so she can tug me away from my mates and into a quick hug that nearly squeezes the life out of me.

"Tandy Lewis," she says, a laugh in her voice as she releases me. "You don't do things by halves, do you?

Can't just be the fated mate to one of these guys. Oh, no. You need two."

I shrug, giving her a teasing smile that does little to hide my relief at her welcome. "You know me, Bil. I've always been too much for one guy."

Out of solidarity with Sierra, I'd thought she'd tell me to take my mates and march my ass right out of her village. Just because she helped them find me, that doesn't mean she wants me here, but as she continues to shake her head, I get the feeling that she does.

"Don't I know it. But now you have two, and I'm sure your mates have made it clear. This is it. Loyalty's big in Sombra."

I nod. "Trust me. I know." Ah, hell. Here goes nothing... "And I'll make sure that, next time Sierra's here, *she* knows that *I* know, too."

Billie smirks. "That said, come here. I want you to meet my mate." She gestures at the green-eyed demon. "This is Glaine. Glaine, this is Tandy."

"You knew my Billie when she was a spawn," Glaine rumbles. "You are her kin, like Sierra is. It is good to meet you, Tandy." His eyes flicker over my shoulder. "I am glad you have finally found your mate," he adds, a touch of reverence to his voice. "If any deserves their forever, it's the doppelseers."

Out of the corner of my eye, I see Lucian nod back. "I am glad to see that you found yours as well, my old friend. Remember, prophecies can change. You just have to make it so."

Damien's purple gaze settles on Billie. "No longer a heart barely used," he says, "but one full of love. Congratulations on your mating, mortal."

"Billie, Damien," I tell him, laying my hand on his arm. "That's Billie—"

"And you're One! Oh my God, I can't believe it!"

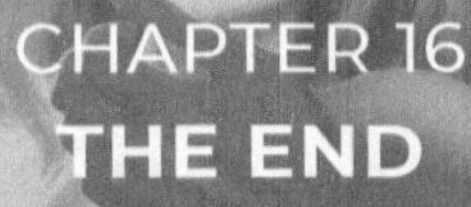

CHAPTER 16
THE END

TANDY

O h. Wow.

Where did she come from?

So fixated on Billie and her mate, I guess I didn't notice that there was another couple standing just behind them. The other demon is in his dark shadowy form, though I can still make out his purple eyes—the same shade as my demons'—and his pair of double horns, just like those Billie's mate has.

The other woman is human, though, and she's not only super pregnant, she's bouncing slightly and clapping her hands as she looks at me.

I want to tell her to stop. Won't that cause damage to the kid? Like, bounce too much, and it might kick-start labor or something?

Then again, I've never been pregnant. Don't really plan on it any time soon, either, so if her mate or even Billie isn't about to stop her, I'll keep my trap shut.

I'd put her about my age, maybe a little younger. She's cute, with her heart-shaped face and wide brown eyes. Her hair is a dark blonde that falls in gentle waves down her back, and her shadowy mate hovers next to her, a silent warning not to upset his pregnant partner.

I step back into the protection of my two mates, then wave. "Hi."

She looks sheepish at my less-than-enthusiastic welcome. "Sorry. Billie said I can come out and meet you, but I needed to be cool after I freaked out meeting Whiskey Rose. But can you blame me? That's Whiskey Rose! But you... you're awesome, too. I mean, One, and... okay." She takes a deep breath, silencing her squeal. "I'll shut up now."

Billie rolls her eyes, but there's no malice in it. In fact, she looks charmed by the other human's reaction, though not even a little surprised.

"This is Kennedy," she tells me. "She's only been in Sombra for about a year in human time, and she was a huge Thr33peat fan growing up."

Wow. I probably should've figured that out when she called me 'One'.

What are the odds? Fate works in funny ways sometimes because here we are: Sierra, Billie, and I were formed into a girl group when we were young teenagers, and now two of the three of us are here in this demon world with a *fan*.

"It's so nice to meet you," I tell Kennedy.

"Are you coming to visit Billie? We have to sit down and chat!"

Billie's forehead furrows. "Your ankles acting up again?"

Kennedy shrugs even as her mate lays his hands on her shoulder, muttering her name softly. Waving him off, she says, "It comes with the territory. I swear, I don't even remember a time I wasn't pregnant, but it's fine. Though I won't say no to a chair right now."

Billie points at one of the houses in the not-too-far distance. "Me and Glaine live closer to this spot than you and Loki. Why don't we bring Tandy in and talk?" She glances over at her mate. "I'm sure you want to speak to the doppelseers, demon. Unless you invited them?"

Damien clears his throat. "The doppelseers offer invitations. We don't seek them."

"But we will accept them anyway," adds Lucian. "Yes. We'd like to speak to the guard. The mage, too," he says, referring to Kennedy's mate. "Loki. Come. You can trust our mate and Glaine's to watch over your female and spawn. We see a healthy birth, all things considered. Your fears are unfounded."

Kennedy reaches behind her, fingers disappearing

into the shadows. "See? Told you. Go with the other guys. I get to finally meet One!"

Part of me wants to tell Lucian and Damien not to leave me with the superfan. It's been a long time since I've had to deal with one, but Lucian nods. "We won't be far, dear one."

Ah, hell. Sure, I made a joke about it after Damien started calling me that, but how did I never notice that Lucian only did after taking my essence and my memories? It's not dear *one*, is it? It's dear *One*...

My mate brushes his claw over my cheek. "If you need us, follow your bond."

"I will, Lucian." Looking over his shoulder, my gaze finds Damien. "Love you."

"Your heart is ours," rumbles Damien.

Sierra had a heart barely used—until she found her demon.

Billie has a heart full of love for her mate.

And me? It belongs to a pair of demon males.

Using our bond, I send him a mental image of the three of us twisted up like pretzels. Lucian's need is like a warm caress, while Damien's is a bonfire.

Now they have a reason not to leave me at the mercy of my old friend and a superfan, I think, as my grin widens. "You know it."

It takes about fifteen minutes before Kennedy inevitably mentions Jared Turner.

I knew it was coming. Even if Billie bit her tongue long enough not to mention that prick, Kennedy would've been the target audience for the tabloids and the gossip rags when the story broke about me 'stealing' Sierra's boyfriend.

Of course she'd want the story straight from the horse's mouth.

Instead of bringing up the long-ago past, I decide to talk about my latest run-in with him. Kennedy squeals again as I tell them both about how Damien went after him, how Lucian and I followed our initial bond to Manhattan, and how I finally got the tiniest bit of revenge on Jared for allowing me take all the credit for screwing everything up when everyone knows it takes two to tango.

Kennedy thought it was hysterical, and once I confirmed that no demons came looking for my mates to clap them in chains, Billie seemed to enjoy hearing about how Jared Turner finally got knocked down a peg or two.

By the end of the story, I can't help but laugh a little myself as I admit, "It was great. Damien had him just about pissing his pants even before he hit him in the head with that stupid award."

"Too bad it wasn't a Grammy," Billie says. "They pack a much bigger punch, according to Sierra."

Before I can ask what she means by that, she gets up from the couch where the three of us have been sitting. Across the front room, there's a window, and she peers out of it.

"Okay. Now, which one is Damien?"

Joining Billie by the the window, I see the four demons standing together: Glaine and Loki on one side, facing off against Lucian and Damien as Lucian says something to the others. I can't hear them, but I know which of my males is mine, even at this distance.

I point at Damien. "The broody, sexy one right there."

Billie frowns slightly. "And Lucian?"

"The sweet, sexy one standing next to Damien."

"So what I'm understanding is you can tell them apart, but they're both sexy," my old friend teases.

Of course. "You can't?"

She blinks at me. "They're identical twins, Tandy. And they're shadows. I'm lucky I can pick out Glaine, and that's only because no one else in Nuit is a soldier with green eyes."

"My mate has purple eyes, too," pipes up the super-fan. "But it's easy to tell Loki apart from other mages because he has two horns."

"Glaine does, too," Billie adds. "It's supposed to mean they're powerful demons." She squints at my mates. "They only have one."

That's not necessarily true. As a pair of twins who

shared their essence their whole lives before giving it to me, technically they do have two pairs of horn. They just each have a pair on their own heads.

Not like I need to one-up Billie and her friend. Maybe a decade ago, I would have, but that's the old Tandy. And while that part of me will never die—especially since I'm immortal now—I don't need to rub it in their faces that my twin mates are the longest-lived, most respected seers in all of Sombra, plus the only set of demons that exist.

Why do that when I can simply give them my most lascivious grin and say, "Who needs two pairs of horns when you have two cocks?"

Kennedy lifts her hand, covering her mouth as she giggles.

Billie—like she used to whenever I made a comment like that as a teen—sighs and rolls her eyes.

I just grin at them.

And that's when, over the sudden, stunned silence, we hear someone shout out near enough to the window to catch our attention.

My mates', too. As one, Damien and Lucian turn in the opposite direction. Loki—two horns with purple eyes—shifts on his heel, racing for the door; no doubt he's coming inside for his pregnant mate. Glaine—two horns with green eyes—starts to jog in the direction that my demons are staring in.

Right. Because he's the guard, and if he's Billie's

mate, he's sure that she can take care of herself. That, or she's safe in the house while he goes to see what's causing the ruckus outside.

I'm sure my mates would want me to do the same. But, thanks to the essence exchange, they have to know that keeping me safe and sound, out of sight and out of mind, is never going to work for me. Hell, I'm the chick who said 'fuck it' and ran into the shadows to find Damien, and even though I understand now just how close to being lost he was when I found him, that didn't stop me from letting him have me however he wanted.

There's a reason why Billie and I always got along. Though Sierra was usually the instigator, with Billie having to bail me and Sierra out whenever we got into trouble, Billie is determined. She's fearless, too, and will never let anyone tell her what to do.

She also has a motherly instinct a mile wide. I'm actually kind of surprised that she's not the one ready to pop out a kid, like Kennedy is—and, from what I understand now, Sierra, too—but she always took care of us. First, Sierra and me while we were in Thr33peat, then Whiskey Rose as Sierra's pop star persona's manager.

Now she has Glaine, and as soon as he takes off, so does she.

I'm curious. Can't help it, and though I wait just long enough to help Kennedy get awkwardly off the couch when she flailed a little, we follow after Billie.

Loki meets us on the front porch leading into Glaine and Billie's home.

"Kennedy," rumbles the purple-eyed demon. "Stay near."

She nods, and the three of us hurry over to where Damien, Lucian, Billie, and Glaine are.

We're not the only ones looking around. Multiple demons—and demonesses that look nothing like the males—step out of their houses, conferring the way that nosy humans do back home.

"What's going on?" asks Kennedy.

"It's Shannon," Loki tells her. Shannon? Who's Shannon? That's a human name if I ever heard one.

Kennedy's hand drops to her belly. "Is it time?"

Her mate nods. "Malphas came running into the village, carrying his human. The clanmother and clan leader went to his quarters. Azazel is there now, too. We must stay here and give them their peace and privacy if we expect the same."

I'm so confused. I mean, yeah, I'm the newbie here, but it's like I'm the only one who has no clue what any of that means.

Even my mates seem to understand. I don't sense any confusion coming from them, and when I turn to find them both, I'm stunned by how absolutely *bright* their eyes are. They're still purple, but like they're suddenly high beams, you'd almost mistake them for white.

"The child is coming," intones Lucian.

"Duke Haures is coming," adds Damien.

"The end is coming," they echo at the same time.

I'm sorry... what?

I just found my demons. What do they mean, the end is coming?

And why, when I reach through the bond to understand what they mean, is desperation to keep me forever the only thing I feel? I thought we had forever—

Something is happening to me. My head feels hazy. My heart is pounding. My fingers are tingling—

The child is coming.

Duke Haures is coming.

Holy fucking shit, if the prophecy that just popped into my head doesn't change like Glaine's must have, *the end is coming.*

As the echoes of my mate's prophecy come skittering down our bond, I shake my head and fist my hips.

The end is coming?

Huh. Not if Tandy Lewis and her doppelseers have anything to say about *that*.

EPILOGUE

MALPHAS

As the first human-demon spawn to be born in this age—the only human-demon child that any living Sombran knows of—it is only fitting that my Shannon and mine's child will arrive on the night of the gold moon.

We knew that they would. The doppelseers foretold our spawn's arrival, knowing that the twin moons of Sombra would be out, the gold one heavy and round as it shed some illumination on our world of shadows. They didn't know the exact gold moon it would be, but every demon can sense the approach of the gold moon instinctively.

After all, during the gold moon, mated males experience mate sickness to a certain degree, whether they are bonded or not. They need their females, and any bond between them is strengthened by an intimate touch when the gods shine down on us through the power of the mystical moon.

Petting your female's cunt. Tasting it. Leaning back as she takes your cock into her mouth, pleasuring it with her tongue... there are ways to be intimate with your mate to silence the mate sickness without making it so that your mate will carry your spawn. But if you do choose to claim your female when the gold moon is at its peak, you will conceive.

I thought my Shannon knew that. With my essence running through her veins, telling her all she needed to know about her Sombra male, I thought she understood. She was the one who welcomed me into her cunt before our deadline ran out that fateful gold moon. I would've ended up trapped in Sammael's enchanted chains, tossed in the demon duke's dungeons by Glaine if Shannon hadn't claimed me with her words, then her cunt later that night.

Now it has been many cycles since I laid my beautiful human out on her bedding, giving her my cock, and creating an immortal bond that will tie us together for the rest of our lives. It has been just as long since the seed I planted in her womb blossomed into something precious. Something that is part of Shannon, part of me, and the spawn I will do anything to protect.

I worship my flower. I did from the moment she ripped me out of my bathtub, summoning me to her human realm, and seasoning me with sage before serenading me by banging one of her cooking utensils against the metal vessel. There isn't anything I won't do for her, and seeing her cradle her belly with one hand while squeezing tightly to mine with the other, I pray to the gods above to allow me to take her pain so that she can birth our child easily.

It's possible. Like how we have a bond that stretches between us, allowing the essence exchange, if Shannon wills her pain to me, I can shoulder it.

We already have a connection. Her colorless hand is wrapped around my red one, the way she's gripping me reminiscent of the red-and-white minty treats that Shannon slipped into my oversized sock—no, I correct, my stocking—that I left out for Santa Claws again this year. She knows they are my favorite, and while I am still rather worried about a jolly prowler sneaking into our quarters while we are asleep, I celebrated the human holiday with her while waiting for our spawn to arrive.

Now they are almost here, and as my mate squeezes my hand tightly before throwing her head back, moaning, I can't wait to meet them.

After another short cry, my mate relaxes against the bedding before gritting out, "I really hope I'm not breaking your fingers."

"You are fine, my mate," I coo, soothing her.

"I mean, you'd deserve it, Mal. You and your magical shadow dick did this to me in the first place, I've been knocked up for two Christmases now, and if that's not bad enough, this kid of ours is too solid to be shadow." My mate blows air out through her nose, rubbing the bottom of her belly. "*Fuck*. These contractions suck ass."

"Give your pain to me." My voice is pleading, and I stay solid myself so that she can grip my hand fully. As my shadows, a touch would give her pleasure, but the way she is sweating along her hairline, I don't know if that would be enough to overwhelm her discomfort. No. It's better that I take it, and Shannon focuses on birthing our child. "Through our bond... with our essence... I shall take it from you."

She narrows her pretty blue eyes at me. "You can do that?"

"I can try."

She exhales roughly, staring up at the ceiling, watching the golden moonlight stream down from one of the holes. "Just don't leave me, Mal. That's all. And if I get nasty when I start to push, just remember that I love you."

Reaching out with a shadowy claw, careful not to scratch her cheek, I turn her so that she has no choice but to look at me. "I adore you, my Shannon. I always will."

Her eyes glisten. After spending so long at my mate's side, it no longer unnerves me that they're dim. In fact, I startle when I approach one of my fellow demons since glowing eyes staring out of a mass of shadows belong to Sombra, and I? Malphas? I belong in Shannon's world with my mate.

We are in Sombra now. As soon as Shannon recognized the signs that our spawn was coming, we opened up the pathway that leads from Jericho to Nuit. It's instinctive now, after all those trips we've taken to meet with the healer, and I was carrying my mate to the house I keep in the village within minutes.

Apollyon and Lilith saw our approach. Lilith came with me so that she could help get Shannon comfortable while Apollyon went in search of Azazel. That was hours ago, and both the clanmother and clan leader have left us to our privacy. Azazel keeps checking on my mate, watching her cunt closely, waiting for a sign that our spawn is crowning before disappearing into the front room.

That, I fear, is my fault. I am her male. Since our bonding, I am the only one who should be blessed with the sight of her cunt, and it took me many cycles to get past my jealousy over the healer needing to look for himself.

I've been good. But between the way his gold eyes gleam as he ducks his head near my Shannon's spread legs and her pained, muffled panting as another contraction hits her, I've found myself growling under my breath in a way that seems to unnerve Azazel.

I have no choice but to swallow the sounds when Shannon's grip on my fingers actually seems to mangle them. "Okay. *Okay.* I don't think that was just a contraction that time. I think this baby is coming *now*."

"Azazel," I bellow.

The healer appears in an instant. He's in his shadows, flying through the open doorway, shifting to his demon form as he crouches down in front of my mate. After a previous warning, he keeps shadows woven around his lower half, but he also adds them as a layer to his claws so that he can reach up and wait to receive our spawn.

I've never watched one be born before. And, my attention solely on my mate as Azazel instructs her to push when he tells her to, I don't see it happen now. I do, however, hear the high-pitched keening cry as our spawn comes into the world.

"It is a female," Azazel announces as he gathers the child up in his shadows.

For a moment, Shannon closes her eyes. Lying back on the birthing nest, she shudders out a relieved breath, then asks in a raw voice, "Where is she? Can I see her?"

Azazel pauses, his back to us. The healer hesitates, and then he murmurs, "Lilith has offered to act as my help. She will clean the afterbirth off and swaddle your spawn while I tend to you, Shannon. Then you can meet your babe."

I want to do so, but I'd prefer to see the healer examine Shannon and make sure my flower is doing well after the birth. I trust the clanmother implicitly, and after spending the last year visiting Nuit, so does Shannon.

While Azazel takes care of my mate, I drop a kiss on her sweaty brow. "You did amazing, my Shannon."

She looks tired yet exhilarated. "I'm so glad she's here. But just in case I haven't told you a million times already? You want to fuck on the gold moon? Use your hand, babe. Kay? I'm one and done."

"One spawn is enough for me," I promise.

"Good."

Shannon closes her eyes, resting while we wait for Lilith to bring our child back to us. Azazel finishes first, declaring that Shannon will need to take three separate herbs, two potions, and sleep as much as possible as a new mother, but other than that, she will recover well.

That is the best news. I'm soaring from hearing that —and that's when Lilith shuffles into the room, holding our newly clean spawn wrapped up in a blanket.

She murmurs her congratulations before offering the spawn to Shannon. Then, as the blanket falls away from our daughter's face, the clanmother slips out of the room.

And I suddenly understand.

Our daughter has my eyes. Bright and gold and glowing healthily, they reflect against her pale skin.

No. Not pale.

Colorless.

I am red. Shannon is white. She would joke that our spawn would be pink. She is part Sombran so, no matter her color, I expected she would be made up of shadows.

She has *none*.

Shannon chuckles, a finger going to the tiny nub on our daughter's brow. "Looks like Amy won the pool. They're not fully developed horns, not yet, but she definitely won't pass for human. 'Course, her eyes are glowing, too. See, Mal? She has your eyes. Your eyes and my skin tone. Ooh, see these tiny little tufts of hair, too? She might just be blonde like her mom."

My lips quirk upward, a small smile at her obvious delight—even as my heart starts racing.

Shannon doesn't realize what this means. When she delves into my essence, she will, but for now, I understand the concern written on Lilith's features, and the hesitation on Azazel's before they left us alone in our quarters.

I understand it, and I refuse to acknowledge it.

This is our spawn, and no matter her appearance, I will love her always.

Azazel bows his head. "I will inform Apollyon that we have a new villager in Nuit."

I would have expected that Lilith would go and tell her mate; both that our child is here, and that she resembles Duke Haures's unique appearance. But if Azazel needs a reason to leave our quarters, that is fair enough.

Besides, there are things I must discuss with my mate that I'd prefer no one else overhear...

I know my mate. Shannon has explained to me her reasons behind the two of us staying in Jericho, the mortal village where she has no clan but for the coffee shop she visits and the bookstore that Loki's female gifted to mine. I am immortal. After the essence exchange, my mate is, too. She will never age. She will never get sick. Never die unless either Duke Haures commands it, or she chooses to end her existence.

She won't. In all my years, I have never met one who is as full of magic as my mate, or with a thirst and joy for life. But that means she will spend the rest of her days in Sombra. Until she must leave, once it is clear that she *is* immortal, she wants to linger in the human world.

Our child changes everything. The wee female will need her mother, and though Duke Haures's first law makes it so that I must forever be Shannon's secret in the mortal world, how can she hide our child?

She might have been able to conceal that she was expecting, but depending on what features of mine our spawn had, and which belonged to her beautiful mother, she would have to be hidden away to keep from breaking Duke Haures' laws—and catching the attention of some of the crueler humans who live in the mortal realm.

There are those in Sombra who will hate my mate and our daughter because of their human blood. Now I see that she looks nothing like a Sombra demon at all—with the exception of the most powerful of us... and before he was the duke, Haures was left to the shadows because of his lack of any. I don't deny that demons can be as cruel as humans, and I only hope that Nuit is free of those bigots.

If not, I have learned much about hunting from Nox. To provide for my mate when we are in Nuit, I barter my art and skills, but Nox reminded me that I have a family to protect. This close to the edge of the shadows, if a demonic creature—one without any essence of their own—attacks, I need to be able to shield Shannon, plus our new daughter.

I will. She may be different from the rest of the worlds, both demon and human, but she is ours, and she is precious.

Shannon's brow is furrowed. Her heart has slowed

its drumming to a more content beat. Our spawn is wrapped in a soft, dark yellow blanket that Shannon packed in her bag before we left our home. She said it reminded her of my eyes, and now it matches the only spot of color on our tiny daughter.

"She's beautiful," whispers my mate.

I brush a claw over her forehead. "Of course, my flower. She is your spawn."

Exhaustion has stolen much of my Shannon's sharp tongue. Her eyes are half-closed, a hum in her throat as she holds our spawn close to her chest. Instead of teasing me, she nods slowly. "She's yours too, Mal. She's ours, baby."

Baby. In Shannon's human language, the word refers to spawn, but when she uses it for me, it's as much a term of endearment as *fiore mi* in Sombran is. She is my flower, I am her 'baby', and our spawn will be—

"Alana."

"What's that?"

Shannon has a list a hundred names long, all of them possible choices for our child. She has them separated by male and female, and of them, only a handful are my suggestions. Part of me was still so surprised that this beautiful creature is my mate. That she lies with me, that she sleeps with me, and that we're building a family together. If she wanted to be in charge of the naming, that is her right as our spawn's mother.

But only during an emotional moment on Christmas Eve, when I showed her the decorating I did as part of her gift—painting a mural of Sombra on one wall of our spawn's future nursery, a mural of New York on another, all so that the child will know they are from both worlds equally no matter where we live— did Shannon admit that she was undecided when it came to our child's name.

She couldn't share her pregnancy with her family. For many cycles, she hid it from her friends. Just like how Duke Haures's first law insists that I am hidden from the mortals in her realm, the same was true of our child. They would be half Sombran no matter what features they received from the both of us, and it was as important to keep the secret of the demon realms from the human world.

I kissed her on the forehead while sitting together next to our indoor, decorated tree, and told her that, when we saw our child, we would know.

And I do.

"Alana," I repeat. "I think we should call her Alana."

Shannon will need to understand that our child is unlike anything I expected. I am Sombran. I *am* shadows.

And my daughter has none.

She will have horns. She has my golden glowing eyes. But the rest of her... she is as colorless as Duke Haures.

Rumors have run for millennia that the duke was blessed by the gods with powers that allow him to rule, but unlike his people, he has no shadows. Neither does our spawn.

What sort of powers have the gods granted her?

"Alana," echoes Shannon. "I like it. It's pretty."

"It's the name of the Queen of Demons," I tell my mate. "Before Duke Haures, we had King Yelios. But before there was a king ruling Sombra, there was Queen Alana, the most powerful demoness to ever live."

Shannon lets out a soft whistle. "History, too. And you think it's fair to name our kid after a legendary queen?"

She has no shadows. I think we must.

"Yes."

"Then Alana it is." Shannon nuzzles the top of the blanket. "My pretty girl. I can't wait to be your mom."

My heart swells. I will ask one of the clan hunters to teach me more than Nox did. I will plead with Apollyon to allow us quarters in the heart of the village. Anything to protect the two females who own *my* heart... I will do anything, I vow, watching Shannon snuggle Alana close.

I don't know how long I do so. Shannon will need

to be moved from the birthing nest to one where she can be more comfortable. Alana will need to be fed, and so will my mate. And, yet, though our world has changed, I cling to this moment for as long as I can... until Apollyon peeks his head hesitantly into our room and, before I can move to stand in front of my mate and my child, he says, "Malphas? Duke Haures is here to meet with you."

Me?

I move in front of the bedding right as Duke Haures, wearing his crystalline crown, comes marching into the room.

I'd expected to go to him. To leave our quarters and greet the duke outside, but there he is, and I'm too stunned to react at first.

"Your grace." I am a simple clan artist. I know of Duke Haures—everyone in Sombra does—but I've never heard of him leaving Mavro for anything, least of all coming to greet a newly born spawn. Spawn are born every day—

—but when Duke Haures's strange blue eyes land on the wrapped bundle in Shannon's arms, his odd features twisting as though he doesn't know what to make of our miracle, I suck in a breath and drop down to one knee, showing our ruler the proper level of respect he would expect from a male with a mate and a child to protect.

He flicks his fingers, clicking his claws together. "Rise, Malphas."

I do. "What an honor to have you here—"

"I came as soon as I was told the child would be born this moon."

Shannon clutches the bundle that is Alana. "Mal? What's going on?"

I wish I knew.

I smile at my mate, then face the imposing ruler again. "Duke Haures. I never expected to see you here in Nuit."

He grins, flashing his tusks. "This is the first time I've visited the outskirts of my domain in centuries. It is your honor, artist. Now, if you would, show me the spawn."

A pulse of refusal comes down our bond. I send reassurance back, then ease toward my mate.

"Trust me," I murmur softly to Shannon.

Her eyes—tired, yet frantic—go wide. But the reassurance reaches her, and she nods. "Support the head, Mal," is all she says as I gently scoop up the bundle.

How did he know? Did Azazel or Apollyon have some way to reach Mavro already, telling Duke Haures of what he'll find in the blankets as I shift my daughter, showing her wee colorless face to our ruler?

I think so because the only reaction Duke Haures gives is a solemn nod.

"Just as it was foretold," he says, his voice booming,

though Alana does nothing but stare curiously at the awe-inspiring demon staring at her. "She is the spawn of the prophecy."

I blink.

Shannon grunts, pushing her aching, tender, raw body up and off of the nest.

And my mate... my love... my *flower*... glares at Duke Haures himself, the lord of Sombra, and says in bewildered human, "What the fuck are you talking about?"

WHAT'S THIS ABOUT A PROPHECY?

So... I'm a mom now.

It's so hard to believe that years have passed since I bought that grimoire from Kennedy's store and summoned Malphas into my apartment. Or that, as a Sombra demon's one true mate, I was knocked up for close to two years before we had our baby girl.

One small problem. Just as I gave birth in Mal's demon village, Duke Haures—the big shot ruler of

Sombra itself—decided to leave his fancy capital city, gracing us with his presence.

Why? Because, turns out, those freaky demon twins had a vision that the birth of the first demon-human kid would either end their world—or save it.

That's a lot to put on the shoulders of anyone, not to mention a baby a couple of hours old. They can't tell me how or why, either, but it doesn't matter. Until the prophecy thing is all cleared up, it looks like Shannon Crewes is living in Sombra full-time now.

I've never spent much time in Mal's world before. With our kid's safety on the line, I'll do what I have to —and anyone who tries to break up my family is going to wish they never crossed this feisty human chick.

For anyone who misses seeing Malphas and Shannon together, who wants to learn about their baby or see what life is like for them years after the first book... this one is for you. It'll have humor, suspense, adventure, and heat, all while readers get to experience Sombra through Shannon's eyes — while also seeing old friends, meeting new ones, and showing that their HEA was only the beginning of their story—and, as the final book in the series, this is the end.

KEEP IN TOUCH

Stay tuned for what's coming up next! Follow me at any of these places—or sign up for my newsletter—for news, promotions, upcoming releases, and more!

SarahSpadeBooks.com
Sarah's Newsletter
Sarah's Signed Book Store

facebook.com/sarahspadebooks
x.com/stressie
instagram.com/sarahspadebooks
amazon.com/author/sarahspade

ALSO BY SARAH SPADE

Holiday Hunk

Halloween Boo

This Christmas

Auld Lang Mine

I'm With Cupid

Getting Lucky

When Sparks Fly

Holiday Hunk: the Complete Series

Claws and Fangs

Leave Janelle

Never His Mate

Always Her Mate

Forever Mates

Hint of Her Blood

Taste of His Skin

Stay With Me

Never Say Never: Gem & Ryker

Bound by the Moon

Sombra Demons

Drawn to the Demon Duke*

Mated to the Monster

Stolen by the Shadows

Santa Claws

Bonded to the Beast

Fated to the Phantom

Claimed by the Creature

Grabbed by the Guard

Taken by the Twins

Shannon in Sombra

Stolen Mates

The Alpha's Heart*

The Feral's Captive

Chase and the Chains

The Beta's Bride

Wolves of Winter Creek

Prey

Pack

Predator

Protector

Sanctuary

Watch Me Burn

Make Me Bleed

Claws Clause

(written as Jessica Lynch)

Mates **free*

Hungry Like a Wolf

Of Mistletoe and Mating

No Way

Season of the Witch

Rogue

Sunglasses at Night

Ain't No Angel

True Angel

Ghost of Jealousy

Night Angel

Broken Wings

Of Santa and Slaying

Lost Angel

Born to Run

Uptown Girl

A Pack of Lies

Here Kitty, Kitty

Ordinance 7304: the Bond Laws (Claws Clause Collection #1)

Living on a Prayer (Claws Clause Collection #2)

Diamonds are a Witch's Best Friend (Claws Clause Collection #3)

9 781961 594418